JULES VERNE's life was characterized by a love for the sea, travel, and adventure. He was born into a family with a seafaring tradition in Nantes, France, in 1828. At an early age he tried to run off and ship out as a cabin boy but was stopped and returned to his family. Verne was sent to Paris to study law, but once there, he quickly fell in love with the theater. He was soon writing plays and opera librettos, and his first play was produced in 1850. When he refused his father's entreaties to return to Nantes and practice law, his allowance was cut off, and he was forced to make his living by selling stories and articles.

Verne combined his gift for exotic narratives with an interest in the latest scientific discoveries. He spent long hours in the Paris libraries studying geology, astronomy, and engineering. Soon he was turning out imaginative stories such as *Five Weeks in a Balloon* (1863) and *Journey to the Center of the Earth* (1864), which were immensely popular all over the world. After *From the Earth to the Moon* (1865), Verne received letters from travelers wishing to sign up for the next lunar expedition. His ability to envision the next stage in man's technological process and his childlike wonder at the possibilities produced *20,000 Leagues Under the Sea* (1870) and *Michael Strogoff* (1876). His biggest success came with *Around the World in Eighty Days* (1872).

Verne's books made him famous and rich. In 1876 he bought a large steam yacht, outfitted with a cabin in which he could write more comfortably than on shore. He sailed from one European port to another and was lionized everywhere he went. His books were widely translated, dramatized, and later filmed. He died at Amiens in 1905.

FROM THE EARTH TO THE MOON

JULES VERNE

Introduction by Gregory Benford

Translated by Lowell Bair

BANTAM CLASSIC

FROM THE EARTH TO THE MOON
A Bantam Book

PUBLISHING HISTORY
From the Earth to the Moon was first published in 1865
Bantam Pathfinder edition published January 1967
Bantam Classic edition / June 1993
Bantam Classic reissue / October 2008

Published by Bantam Dell
A Division of Random House, Inc.
New York, New York

Bantam Books and the rooster colophon are registered trademarks of
Random House, Inc.

ISBN 978-0-553-21420-8

Printed in the United States of America
Published simultaneously in Canada

www.bantamdell.com

OPM   21   20   19   18   17   16   15

CONTENTS

CHAPTER 25

CHAPTER 26

CHAPTER 27

CHAPTER 28

INTRODUCTION:

THE EXACT DREAMER

WONDER—THAT is the key to understanding Jules Verne, the first novelist to claim excitement and awe as his territory. Because he wrote with a sure sense of the wonders that lay beyond everyday life, Verne was considered a children's writer. But his work has outlasted vast numbers of "serious" novels about character and setting that are now mere historical curiosities.

We live in a time when the first expedition to the moon, in 1969, is a fading memory. Why, then, read about past visions of flying to the moon? After all, we know how it really happened—the ending is no surprise.

Verne's answer would be, "Because the sense of *possibility* must be kept alive." Unlike yesterday's yellowing newspapers, the quality of wonder does not fade. Verne believed wonder to be an emotion that grows out of our sense of adventure and inspires us to reach our fullest potential. Though men have now traveled to the moon, the ideas and attitudes Jules Verne packed into *From the Earth to the Moon* are still alive today. And the novel even contains a prediction that may yet be fulfilled.

Verne invented modern science fiction. Others had written fantastic novels and stories using elements of science, such as Mary Shelley's dark, brooding gothic novel,

Frankenstein. But Jules Verne devised *science fiction*—stories with the scientific content in the foreground, as much a character as any person. More than any other figure of the nineteenth century, he saw the possibilities of the soaring century to come—and actually made things happen by igniting the imaginations of people everywhere.

For decades Verne was the best known of all French authors, valued not so much for his plots but for his ideas. He labored to infuse his novels with the feeling that these events *could* happen no matter how impossible they seemed at first glance. *From the Earth to the Moon,* first published in 1865, provides some excellent examples of this technique.

Verne had great faith in the growing potential of the still-young United States, and often predicted that it would lead the world in the following century. So when thinking about going to the moon, Verne picked the United States for his setting. "The Yankees, the world's best mechanics, are engineers the way Italians are musicians and Germans are metaphysicians: by birth." He wrote the book while the bloodiest battles of the Civil War still raged, yet was able to look beyond the ongoing American agony and envision a postwar future.

The members of the fictional Baltimore Gun Club are restless for activity. Its leader, the man with a grand idea—a typical Verne hero—is an anomaly at the Gun Club: "all his limbs were intact." The image of hobbled veterans making a huge leap to another world is Verne's way of showing how limitations can be overcome—by work, will, and wonder. His Gun Club dreamers, aware of the latest scientific developments, know that the mathematician Carl Gauss has already proposed signaling to possible inhabitants of the moon and Mars by building giant stone triangles on the earth that could be seen from a vast distance. But mere signals would not be enough for Verne's heroes, who feel in their bones that by dreaming as exactly—as precisely and scientifically—as possible, they can live up to the full possibilities of their lives. This basic theme lights up over a hundred of his "extraordinary voyage" novels.

But the members of the Baltimore Gun Club aren't the usual run of aimless, romantic nineteenth-century dreamers. Verne's men—this was long before women aspired to such things—are relentlessly practical. Early on they consider a story by Edgar Allan Poe (a writer Verne admired) in which a man floats to the moon in "a balloon filled with a gas drawn from nitrogen and thirty-seven times lighter than hydrogen." This is an insider's joke. Nitrogen, the most plentiful gas in our own atmosphere, is already far heavier than hydrogen. Nobody could "extract" a lighter gas from it without breaking up the atoms—and still it would be heavier than hydrogen.

Here and elsewhere Verne mocks his era's great interest in balloon sailing to the planets. It is now hard to comprehend that most people of that time had no idea what "outer space" meant. To them, balloons—which had just begun to be used to fly—were a logical way to travel to the crescent they could plainly see waiting in the sky. They never doubted that there would be air available throughout such a journey—wasn't there plenty of it here? Balloons rise because they contain gases lighter than air. Few popular writers realized that because space is a vacuum, this doesn't work.

In 1865 there were five other books on interplanetary themes published in French, including *Voyage to Venus, An Inhabitant of the Planet Mars, Voyage to the Moon,* and even a survey by an astronomer, *Imaginary Moons and Real Moons*. All featured balloons. One writer did have a dim idea of using rockets, but his squirted water out the end, not fiery gas. Then he ruined the effect by thriftily collecting and reusing the ejected water. Common sense should have told him that such a ship would gain no momentum: The water's push would be canceled when the water was caught. (The recycling squirter idea seems to have had a lingering appeal; it was proposed as late as 1927 by an engineer.)

Verne made fun of the invention, saying that his own launch mechanism, a cannon, would certainly work. No suspicious mechanics for him! He stuck with engineering he knew would work—artillery, the workhorse of battle. The story proceeds with an engineer's relish for the details, the numbers, the tug of technical arguments. Verne checked his calculations with experts. When the numbers told him that the shell of a capsule would be impossibly heavy if made of iron, he decided to use aluminum, which then was rare and costly, unheard of as a construction material. (One wonders what he would have thought of our soft-drink cans.) This was Verne's secret—showing the wonder lurking behind the mask of gritty particulars.

He used this same method to invent many of the amazing details that now strike us as so prescient. Since the United States was the most likely nation to undertake so bold a venture, where would his veterans place the cannon? Verne describes attaining the right "plane of the ecliptic," which is a reasonable motivation but sidesteps the more detailed logic behind his choice of launch site. He knew that to artillery gunners, the earth's rotation is important in predicting where a shell will land—while it is in flight, the land moves beneath it. In aiming for the moon, there's an even bigger effect. Think of the earth as a huge merry-go-round. If you stand at the north pole, the earth spins under your feet but you don't move at all. Stand on the equator, though, and the earth swings you around at a speed of about a thousand miles an hour. You don't feel it because the air is moving too.

But that speed matters a lot if you're aiming to leap into orbit. Verne had the crucial idea right—that *escape velocity* is the key to getting away from the earth's gravitational pull. The added boost from the earth's rotation led him to believe that the American adventurers would seek a spot as close to the equator as possible, while still keeping within their national territory. A glance at the map told him that the obvious sites were in Texas and Florida.

This is exactly what happened in the American space program nearly a century later, when the launch site of the Apollo program became a political football between Texas and Florida. Florida won, as Verne predicted, but not for political reasons. NASA engineers wanted their rocket stages to fall harmlessly into the ocean. Verne picked Stone Hill, on almost the exact latitude as Cape Kennedy, the Apollo launch site.

Similarly, he correctly foretold the shape of the capsule, the number of astronauts (three), weightlessness in space, a splashdown at sea picked up by the American Navy, and even the use of rockets to change orbit and return to earth. These last three details come from the book's sequel, *Around the Moon,* which Verne published five years after *From the Earth to the Moon.* It takes up the voyage itself, which swings around the moon and returns. There are errors, too, such as a scene in which the astronauts simply open a window on what should have been a vacuum and toss out a dead dog.

The biggest error in Verne's calculations is the cannon itself. At the acceleration needed to reach the earth's escape velocity of seven miles *per second,* the force would have smeared the hearty astronauts into a thin, bloody paste. Verne always tended to minimize problems in dynamics. He felt that by the time engineers could build his imaginary machines, they would have a lot of new tricks up their sleeves. These would make matters easier than they seemed in Verne's own time. In this he was right—a true moon-rocket launch imposes only a few times the earth's gravitational acceleration ("gees") on the passengers.

Nevertheless, his moon-launching cannon is an embarrassment. Verne's adventurers would have been squashed. He gives them some help with a water shock absorber, and discusses it in detail. But he must have known that it would not have helped much.

It is a bit curious why Verne chose this brute-force method when the rocket was known to him—though only as a minor military weapon and as fireworks. When he wrote *Around the Moon,* he showed that he indeed understood the principles of rocketry, since he let his capsule fire several to propel it back to earth. Verne probably wanted the luscious specifics of artillery to light up his story—to ground it in reality. People knew that cannons worked with awful efficiency. Rockets would have seemed to his audience rather odd, speculative, and unlikely.

Then again, maybe Verne was not so far wrong about artillery and outer space—only he saw further into the future than our time. Although rockets opened the space frontier, through the inventions of the American Robert Goddard (an ardent Verne fan), cannons are making a comeback.

In 1991 the U.S. government began a research program aiming to deliver payloads into orbit around the earth at a low price—by using guns. The barrel, reinforced by steel and concrete, is a narrow pipe about three hundred feet long. An explosion starts the process, driving hydrogen gas against the underside of a bullet-shaped capsule. The goal is to place a capsule in orbit within three years. Once there, it will use rockets to maneuver itself into a proper, nearly circular orbit about the earth—just as Verne predicted.

Why now, nearly 130 years after *From the Earth to the Moon*, are we finally exploring the full potential of industrial-age technology? The trick is that only computer-age engineering can deal with the massive acceleration—thousands of times the earth's "gee." We now know how to make tiny circuits in rock-solid silicon. We have rockets with hard-packed chemical fuel.

Nothing in the capsule will be free to break loose and smash into the rest of the extremely compact "spaceship." Its instruments will be fitted together at extremely fine tolerances, with not a hairbreadth of misalignment or wasted space. This is so that the engineers can pack into a few pounds the capability to look down and monitor the earth's environment, take readings of the conditions in orbit, and even gaze outward through fine-ground lenses to study other worlds. Such capability must be crammed into a short tube that can pass through a narrow barrel about an inch wide.

With further engineering it seems possible to send these solid ambassadors to probe other planets, and the moon too. They would be much cheaper than present spacecraft. Firing them into orbit (with a huge bang that would have gratified Verne) will cost about one percent of the price of putting a pound in orbit using our present shuttle craft.

One of the book's chapter titles, "The Hymn to the

Projectile," is almost a parody of Verne's reverence for technology. His J. T. Maston rhapsodizes, "Would you like figures? I'll give you some eloquent ones!"—and reels off the specifications on gunpowder and mass, a poetry of arithmetic unique to Verne. He reasoned that people can be convinced of the reality of a possibility only if it is described with great specificity. His characters are masters of geometry: "Here and there he wrote a pi or an x^2. He even appeared to extract a certain cube root with the greatest of ease."

They know their guns too. Their huge construction "will be a cannon, since its chamber will have the same diameter as its bore; it will be a howitzer, since it will fire a hollow shell; and it will be a mortar, since it will be elevated at an angle of ninety degrees..." One of the best ways to convince your readers that you are a reliable narrator is to tell them something about their own world—such as the distinctions between types of artillery—that they didn't know before. (Verne handed this strategy down to the countless authors of today who tell us how hotels, airports, battleships, hospitals, or law firms work, all in relentless, telling detail.)

This isn't merely Verne's enthusiasm overpowering his story. Rather, it marks the birth of "hard" science fiction, the variety that stays loyal to the facts, as nearly as the author knows them. Hard sf also describes the way engineers and scientists actually work: no lonely experimenters on mountaintops, inventing Frankensteins out of dead body parts; no easy improvising to get around tough problems—Verne's tinkerers work in groups, argue, make hard choices. Audiences of his time found such detail gripping and convincing.

Writers such as Arthur C. Clarke (*2001: A Space Odyssey*), Robert A. Heinlein, and the other master sf writer of the nineteenth century, H. G. Wells, followed in this tradition. Verne influenced even those who didn't quite know who he was. Isaac Asimov once told me that when he was still a young science fiction fan he found himself listening to a lecture about a great foreign writer, a master of fantastic literature. But Asimov couldn't recognize the name. Giving the French pronunciation, the lecturer said, "Surely you must know Zueel Pfern," and described *From the Earth to the Moon.* Asimov replied in his Brooklyn accent, "Oh, you mean Jewels Voine!"

I had a similar experience, not realizing for years that Verne was not an American—after all, he set so many of his stories in the United States. In tribute, I named a character in my first hard sf novel, *Jupiter Project,* after one of his.

Verne died only a few months before the Wright brothers' first flight at Kitty Hawk, North Carolina. But he had seen such flights in his mind's eye decades before, and the brothers had read his novels. We can get a feeling for his faith in the long-range possibilities of humanity from the remarkable memorial his son placed over his grave. It shows Verne with hair streaming, as if he were in flight, breaking free of his shroud and tomb, rising up magnificently from the dead. Above it are simply his name and the words *Onward to immortality and eternal youth.* It's hard to be more optimistic than that.

Hard sf is often optimistic, but it is not unsophisticated. Verne slips in plenty of humor that makes light-hearted fun of his adventurers. When they discuss whether other planets could be inhabited and mention that the tilt of the earth's axis makes for some violent weather, an enthusiastic voice cries, "Let's unite our efforts, invent machines, and straighten out the earth's axis!"

In addition to great scientific and technological advances, Verne foresaw many bleak aspects of our century—total war, industrial squalor, social dislocations. But he always saw fresh possibility looming beyond the troubles. Many of his inventions "came true," whereas the other great founder of modern science fiction, H. G. Wells, played a bit looser with the facts and their implications. When Wells followed Verne, writing *The First Men in the Moon* (1901), he got his astronauts there with a metal that simply did away with the law of gravity—presto! Verne said dismissively, "I make use of physics. He invents . . . Show me this metal. Let him produce it!"

Ever since he was a struggling writer, Verne intended to ground his fiction in scientific fact. Reflecting upon his ambitions in 1856, he wrote in his journal: "Not mere poetry, but analytic fantasy. Something monomaniacal. Things playing a more important part than people, love giving way to deduction and other sources of ideas, style, subject, interest. The basis of the novel transferred from the heart to the head . . ."

This attention to detail, balanced by Verne's soaring imagination, makes the book in your hands still exciting. He published it in the last year of the American Civil War, 1865, 104 years before we voyaged to the moon. By reliving the visions of yesterday, it teaches us a lot about *why* people spin great dreams. His characters seek to expand human horizons—both physical and conceptual.

And what dreams Verne had! We can grasp how much he changed the world by recalling real events that appeared first as acts of imagination in his novels. The American submarine *Nautilus,* its name taken from *20,000 Leagues Under the Sea,* surfaced at the north pole and its captain (not named Nemo, alas) talked by radio with President Eisenhower less than a century after the novel was published. The explorer Haroun Tazieff, a Verne fan who had read *Journey to the Center of the Earth,* climbed down into the rumbling throat of a volcano in Africa, seeking secrets of the earth's core. An Italian venturer coasted over the icy Arctic wastes in a dirigible just as Verne proposed. A French explorer crawled into the caves of southern Europe, stumbled upon the ancient campgrounds of early man, and stood before underground lakes where mammoths once roasted over crackling fires—as Verne had envisioned. In 1877 Verne foresaw a journey through the entire solar system, a feat accomplished by NASA's robot voyagers a century later.

So he endures. Many of his precisely envisioned dreams will never find an echo in actual events. But Jules Verne saw huge possibility when others saw mere social mannerisms—the great concern of most nineteenth-century novels.

Perhaps we can learn this from him: that potential lasts longer than details of the moment. And that wonder works.

Gregory Benford

November 1992

CHAPTER 1

THE GUN CLUB

DURING THE Civil War in the United States an influential club was formed in Baltimore. The vigor with which the military instinct developed in that nation of shipowners, merchants, and mechanics is well known. Shopkeepers left their counters and became captains, colonels, and generals without ever having gone to West Point. They soon equaled their Old World colleagues in the "art of war" and, like them, won victories by lavishly expending ammunition, money, and men.

But in the science of ballistics the Americans far surpassed the Europeans. Not that their guns attained a higher degree of perfection, but they were made much larger and therefore reached much greater ranges. When it comes to grazing fire, plunging fire, direct fire, oblique fire, or raking fire, the English, French, and Prussians have nothing to learn, but their cannons, howitzers, and mortars are only pocket pistols compared to the awesome engines of the American artillery.

This should surprise no one. The Yankees, the world's best mechanics, are engineers the way Italians are musicians and Germans are metaphysicians: by birth. Nothing could then be more natural than for them to bring their bold ingenuity to the science of ballistics. The wonders performed in this domain by men like Parrott,

Dahlgren, and Rodman are known to everyone. Armstrong, Paliser, and Treuille de Beaulieu could only bow to their transatlantic rivals.

And so during the terrible struggle between the North and the South the artillerymen reigned supreme. The Union newspapers enthusiastically extolled their inventions, and there was no tradesman so humble, no idler so guileless that he did not rack his brain day and night calculating fantastic trajectories.

Now when an American has an idea he looks for another American who shares it. If there are three of them they elect a president and two vice presidents. If there are four they appoint a secretary and their staff is ready to function. If there are five they convene in a general assembly and their club is formed. That was how it happened in Baltimore. A man who had invented a new cannon associated himself with the man who had cast it and the man who had bored it. That was the nucleus of the Gun Club. A month after its formation it had 1,833 resident members and 30,575 corresponding members.

There was one strict condition for membership in the club: the applicant had to have invented or at least improved a cannon; or if not a cannon, some other kind of firearm. But it must be said that inventors of fifteen-shot revolvers, pivoting rifles, or saber pistols were not held in high esteem. The artillerymen took precedence over them in all circumstances.

"The respect they get," one of the most learned orators of the Gun Club said one day, "is proportional to the mass of their cannons and in direct ratio to the square of the distances reached by their projectiles." This was almost a psychological application of Newton's law of gravity.

Once the Gun Club had been founded, it was easy to imagine the results produced by the Americans' inventive genius. Their cannons took on colossal proportions, and their projectiles reached out beyond all normal limits to cut harmless strollers in half. All these inventions outstripped the timid instruments of European artillery, as the following figures will show.

In the "good old days," a 36-pound cannon ball would go through 36 horses and 68 men at a distance of 100 yards. The art was still in its infancy. It has come a long way since then. The Rodman cannon, which shot a projectile weighing half a ton to a distance of seven miles, could easily have flattened 150 horses and 300 men. The Gun Club considered testing this, but while the horses raised no objection to the experiment, it was unfortunately impossible to find men willing to take part in it.

Be that as it may, these cannons had extremely murderous effects. With each of their shots, combatants fell like wheat before the scythe. Compared to such projectiles what was the famous cannon ball which put twenty-five men out of action at Coutras in 1587, or the one that killed forty infantrymen at Zorndorf in 1758, or the Austrian cannon that felled seventy enemy soldiers each time it was fired at Kesseldorf in 1742? What was the amazing gunfire at Jena or Austerlitz, which decided the outcome of the battle? There was *real* artillery in the Civil War! At the battle of Gettysburg a conical projectile shot from a rifled cannon struck down 173 Confederates, and during the crossing of the Potomac a Rodman ball sent 215 Southerners into an obviously better world. We must also mention the formidable mortar invented by J. T. Maston, distinguished member and permanent secretary of the Gun Club. It was more lethal than any of the others, for it killed 337 people the first time it was fired, though it is true that it did so by bursting.

What can we add to these figures, so eloquent in themselves? Nothing. It will therefore be easy to accept the calculation made by the statistician Pitcairn: he divided the number of members in the Gun Club by the number of victims of their cannon balls and found that each member had killed an average of 2,375 and a fraction men.

From this figure it is clear that the aims of that learned society were the destruction of the human race for philanthropical reasons and the improvement of war weapons, regarded as instruments of civilization. It was an assemblage of Angels of Death who at the same time were thoroughly decent men.

It must be added that these dauntless Yankees did not confine themselves to theory: they also acquired direct, practical experience. Among them were officers of all ranks, from lieutenant to general, soldiers of all ages, some who had just begun their military career and others who had grown old over their gun carriages. Many fell on the field of battle, and their names were inscribed on the Gun Club's honor roll. Most of those who came back bore the marks of their unquestionable valor. Crutches, wooden legs, artificial arms with iron hooks at the wrist, rubber jaws, silver skulls, platinum noses—nothing was lacking in the collection. The aforementioned Pitcairn calculated that in the Gun Club there was not quite one arm for every four men, and only one leg for every three.

But these valiant artillerymen paid little heed to such trifles, and they felt rightfully proud when a battle report showed the number of casualties to be ten times as great as the number of projectiles used.

One day, however, one sad and wretched day, the survivors of the war made peace. The shooting gradually died down; the mortars fell silent; muzzled howitzers and drooping cannons were taken back to their arsenals; cannon balls were piled up in parks; bloody memories faded; cotton grew magnificently in abundantly fertilized fields; mourning clothes and the grief they represented began to wear thin, and the Gun Club was plunged in idle boredom.

A few relentless workers still made ballistic calculations and went on dreaming of gigantic, incomparable projectiles. But without opportunities for practical application these theories were meaningless, and so the rooms of the Gun Club became deserted, the servants dozed in the antechambers, the newspapers gathered dust on the tables, sounds of sad snoring came from the dark corners, and the members, once so noisy, now reduced to silence by a disastrous peace, lethargically abandoned themselves to visions of platonic artillery.

"It's disheartening!" the worthy Tom Hunter said one evening while his wooden legs were slowly charring in front of the fireplace in the smoking room. "There's nothing to do, nothing to hope for! What a tedious life! Where are the days when we were awakened every morning by the joyful booming of cannons?"

"Those days are gone," replied the dashing Bilsby, trying to stretch his missing arms. "How wonderful they were! You could invent a howitzer and try it out on the enemy as soon as it was cast, then when you came back to camp you'd get a word of praise from Sherman or a handshake from McClellan! But now the generals have become shopkeepers again, and balls of yarn are the deadliest projectiles they're likely to deal with. The future is bleak for artillery in America!"

"You're right, Bilsby, it's a cruel disappointment!"

said Colonel Bloomsberry. "One day you give up your calm, peaceful life, you learn the manual of arms, you leave Baltimore and march off to battle, you fight heroically, and then, two or three years later, you have to lose the fruit of all your efforts and do nothing but stand around idly with your hands in your pockets."

The valiant colonel would have been unable to demonstrate his own idleness in this way, though not from lack of pockets.

"And no war in sight!" said the famous J. T. Maston, scratching his rubber skull with the iron hook at the end of his arm. "There's not even a cloud on the horizon, and yet there's still so much to be done in the science of artillery! Only this morning I drew up a complete set of plans of a mortar that's destined to change the laws of war!"

"Really?" said Tom Hunter, involuntarily recalling the test firing of Maston's last creation.

"Yes," said Maston. "But what good did it do me to make all those studies and work out all those difficulties? I was only wasting my time. The New World seems determined to live in peace, and the belligerent *New York Tribune* has begun predicting catastrophes caused by the scandalous growth of the population."

"But there's always a war going on in Europe to support the principle of nationality," said Colonel Bloomsberry.

"What of it?"

"Well, there might be something for us to do over there, and if our services were accepted..."

"What!" cried Bilsby. "Are you suggesting that we do ballistic research for foreigners?"

"It would be better than not doing any at all," retorted the colonel.

"Yes, it would," said J. T. Maston, "but it's out of the question."

"Why?"

"Because in the Old World they have ideas about promotion that are contrary to all our American habits. They think a man can't become a general unless he's first been a second lieutenant, which is the same as saying that you can't be a good gunner unless you've cast the gun yourself! It's . . ."

"Ridiculous, that's what it is!" said Tom Hunter, stabbing the arm of his chair with his Bowie knife. "But since that's how things are, there's nothing left for us to do but plant tobacco or distill whale oil!"

"Do you mean to say," J. T. Maston exclaimed in a ringing voice, "that the last years of our lives will not be devoted to the improvement of firearms? That there will be no new opportunities to test the range of our projectiles? That the air will never again be bright with the flash of our cannons? That there will be no international difficulties which will enable us to declare war on some transatlantic country? That the French will never sink a single one of our steamers, or that the English will never hang any of our citizens in direct violation of the law of nations?"

"No, Maston," replied Colonel Bloomsberry, "we'll never be that lucky. Not one of those things will happen, and even if one of them did happen, it wouldn't do us any good! Americans are getting less and less touchy all the time. It won't be long before we're a nation of old women!"

"We're becoming humble," said Bilsby.

"And we're being humbled!" added Tom Hunter.

"It's all too true!" J. T. Maston said with renewed vehemence. "There are all kinds of reasons for fighting, but we don't fight! We're intent on saving arms and legs for people who don't know what to do with them! And there's no need to look very far for a reason for going to war. For example, America once belonged to England, didn't it?"

"Yes, it did," replied Tom Hunter, angrily poking the fire with the end of his crutch.

"Well, then," said J. T. Maston, "why shouldn't it be England's turn to belong to America?"

"That would be only fair," said Colonel Bloomsberry.

"Just go and suggest it to the President!" said J. T. Maston. "You'll see what kind of a reception he'll give you!"

"It wouldn't be a very polite reception," Bilsby murmured between the four teeth he had saved from battle.

"I certainly won't vote for him in the next election!" said J. T. Maston.

"Neither will I!" the bellicose cripples all shouted at once.

"Meanwhile," said the intrepid J. T. Maston, "if I'm not given a chance to try out my mortar on a real battlefield, I'll resign from the Gun Club and go off into the wilds of Arkansas."

"And we'll all go with you!" replied the others.

Things had reached this point, the members of the Gun Club were becoming more and more wrought up, and the club was threatened with dissolution when an unexpected event forestalled that catastrophe.

The day after the conversation reported above, each member of the club received the following notice:

Baltimore, October 3
The President of the Gun Club has the honor of
informing his colleagues that during the meeting

on October 5, he will make an announcement that will be of the greatest interest to them. He therefore strongly urges them to be present.

Impey Barbicane
President

CHAPTER 2

PRESIDENT BARBICANE'S
ANNOUNCEMENT

A T EIGHT o'clock on the evening of October 5, a dense crowd was milling in the rooms of the Gun Club at 21 Union Square. All the members who lived in Baltimore had responded to their president's invitation. As for the corresponding members, express trains were bringing them in by the hundreds and they were pouring through the streets of the city. Large though the meeting hall was, it was unable to hold this influx of learned members, and so they overflowed into the adjoining rooms, the halls, and even into the grounds outside. There they encountered the ordinary people who were swarming around the doors, each one trying to make his way to the front, all eager to learn what President Barbicane's important announcement was going to be, pushing, jostling, and crushing one another with the freedom of action that is peculiar to a populace that has been raised with the idea of self-government.

That evening a stranger in Baltimore would have been unable to enter the meeting hall no matter how much he might have been willing to pay. It was reserved exclusively for the resident and corresponding members of the Gun Club, and no one else was admitted into it. Even the local dignitaries and the members of the city government had to mingle with the crowd and try to catch word of what was taking place inside.

Meanwhile the meeting hall presented a curious spectacle. This immense room was wonderfully well adapted to its purpose. Tall pillars composed of superposed cannons resting on bases of thick mortars supported the lacy wrought-iron reinforcements of the ceiling. The walls were adorned with clusters of blunderbusses, arquebuses, muskets, carbines, and all other kinds of firearms, ancient and modern. Gas blazed from a thousand revolvers grouped in the form of chandeliers; the magnificent lighting was completed by candelabra composed of pistols and rifles. Models of cannons, samples of bronze, sighting marks shot full of holes, metal plates shattered by the cannon balls of the Gun Club, collections of rammers and sponges, strings of bombs, necklaces of projectiles, garlands of shells—in short, all the tools of the artilleryman, surprised the eye by their astonishing arrangements and gave one to understand that their real purpose was more decorative than murderous.

In the place of honor, sheltered by a beautiful glass case, was a broken twisted fragment of a breech. This was a precious relic of J. T. Maston's mortar.

At the far end of the room, the president of the club, attended by four secretaries, occupied a broad esplanade. His seat, resting on a sculptured gun carriage, had the massive shape of a thirty-two-inch mortar. It was pointed at a ninety-degree angle and suspended on trunnions, so that the president could give it a rocking motion that was quite pleasant in hot weather. The desk was an enormous iron plate supported by six carronades. On it was an exquisite inkpot made from a tastefully engraved canister shot, and a bell that could be made to detonate like a pistol. During heated discussions this unusual bell was hardly loud enough to be heard above the voices of the excited artillerymen.

In front of the desk, benches arranged in zigzags like the circumvallations of a fortification, formed a series of bastions and curtains in which the members of the Gun Club took their places, and that evening it could have been truly said that the ramparts were manned. The members knew their president well enough to be sure that he would not have disturbed them without a reason of the greatest importance.

Impey Barbicane was a calm, cold, austere man of forty, with an eminently serious and concentrated mind; accurate as a chronometer, with a robust constitution and an unshakable character; adventurous though not chivalrous, bringing practical ideas into even his most daring ventures; a perfect example of the New Englander, the colonizing northerner, the descendant of the Roundheads who were so baneful to the Stuarts, the implacable enemy of the southern gentlemen, those American Cavaliers. In short, he was a dyed-in-the-wool Yankee.

He had made a fortune in the lumber business. When he was placed in charge of the artillery during the war, he showed himself to be fertile in inventions. Bold in his ideas, he made great contributions to progress in artillery, and gave a powerful impetus to experimental work.

He was a man of average size, but there was one thing about him that made him a rare exception in the Gun Club: all his limbs were intact. His strongly marked features seemed to have been drawn with a square and a scriber. If it is true that, to discern a man's instincts, one must look at him from the side, Barbicane's profile gave all the signs of determination, boldness, and coolheadedness.

He was now sitting motionless and silent in his chair,

thoughtful, apparently oblivious to everything around him, sheltered beneath his stovepipe hat, one of those black silk cylinders that seem to be screwed onto American skulls.

His colleagues were talking loudly around him without distracting him. They questioned one another, made suppositions, scrutinized their president, and vainly tried to solve the mystery of his imperturbable face.

When the detonating clock in the meeting hall struck eight, Barbicane suddenly stood up as though he were moved by a spring. A hush fell over the hall and he began speaking in a rather grandiloquent tone:

"Worthy colleagues, for too long now a sterile peace has kept the members of the Gun Club in deplorable idleness. After a period of several years that were filled with action, we had to abandon our work and stop short on the road to progress. I do not hesitate to say openly that any war which would bring our weapons back to us would be welcome."

"Yes, war!" cried the impetuous J. T. Maston.

He was answered by shouts of "Hear, hear!" from all over the hall.

"But under present circumstances, war is impossible," Barbicane went on, "and despite the hopes of my honorable interrupter, many long years will go by before our cannons again thunder on a battlefield. We must accept this fact and seek another outlet for our restless energy."

His listeners sensed that he was approaching a crucial point. They redoubled their attention.

"For several months I have been wondering whether, without going outside our specialty, we might not undertake some great experiment worthy of the nineteenth century, and whether progress in ballistics might not enable us to bring it to a successful conclusion. I have reflected, worked, and calculated, and my studies have convinced me that we must be successful in a project that would seem impractical in any other country. This carefully planned project is the subject of my address to you this evening. It is worthy of you and of the Gun Club's past, and it cannot fail to make a great noise in the world."

"A great noise?" asked an excited artilleryman.

"Yes, in the true sense of the word," replied Barbicane.

"Don't interrupt!" said several voices.

"Please give me your full attention," said Barbicane.

A quiver ran through the whole audience. After quickly pulling down his hat more firmly, Barbicane continued his speech in a calm voice:

"There is not one of you, my friends, who has not seen the moon or at least heard of it. Do not be surprised that I should talk to you about the moon. It is perhaps reserved for us to be the Columbuses of that unknown world. If you will understand my plan and do everything in your power to help carry it out, I will lead you in the conquest of the moon, and its name will be added to those of the thirty-six states that form this great nation!"

"Hurrah for the moon!" the Gun Club shouted in a single voice.

"The moon has been intensely studied," said Barbicane. "Its mass, density, weight, volume, composition, movements, distance, and role in the solar system have been accurately determined. Maps have been drawn of it with a precision that equals or surpasses that of maps of the earth. Beautiful photographs have been taken of it. In a word, we know everything about it that the mathematical sciences, astronomy, geology, and optics can teach us. But so far there has never been any direct communication with it."

These words were greeted with a surge of interest and surprise.

"Allow me to remind you in a few words of how certain ardent minds set off on imaginary journeys and claimed to have discovered the secrets of our satellite. In the seventeenth century a man named David Fabricius boasted of having seen the inhabitants of the moon with his own eyes. In 1649, a Frenchman, Jean Baudoin, published his *Journey to the World of the Moon, by Domingo Gonzáles, Spanish Adventurer.* At about the same time, Cyrano de Bergerac wrote the account of a lunar expedition that became so popular in France. Later, Fontenelle, another Frenchman—the French are greatly concerned with the moon—wrote *The Plurality of Worlds,* a masterpiece in its time. But the march of science crushes even masterpieces! Some time around 1835, a pamphlet translated from the *New York American* appeared in France. It told how Sir John Herschel, having been sent to the Cape of Good Hope to make some astronomical studies, had brought the moon to an apparent distance of eighty yards with a telescope improved by internal lighting. He was said to have clearly seen caves with hippopotamuses living in them, green mountains fringed with gold lace, sheep with ivory horns, white deer, and inhabitants with membraneous wings like that of a bat. This pamphlet, the work of an American named Locke, caused a great commotion for a time, but it was soon recognized as a hoax, and the French were the first to laugh."

"Laughing at an American!" cried J. T. Maston. "Why, that's grounds for war!"

"Be calm, my good friend. Before they laughed, the French were completely taken in by our compatriot. To bring this quick historical sketch to an end, I shall add that Hans Pfaal of Rotterdam, traveling in a balloon filled with a gas drawn from nitrogen and thirty-seven times lighter than hydrogen, reached the moon in nineteen days.

This journey, like those I have previously mentioned, was purely imaginary, but it was the work of a strange, contemplative genius who was also a popular American writer. I am referring to Edgar Allan Poe!"

"Hurrah for Edgar Allan Poe!" shouted the assembly, electrified by his words.

"So much for those purely literary efforts, which are completely incapable of establishing any serious relations with the moon. I must add, however, that several practical minds have tried to enter into communication with it. A few years ago, for example, a German geometer proposed that a committee of scientists be sent to the Steppes of Siberia. There on a vast plain, by means of reflectors, they would lay out immense geometric figures, including the square of the hypotenuse. 'Any intelligent being,' said the geometer, 'will understand the scientific purpose of that figure. The inhabitants of the moon, if there are any, will reply with a similar figure, and once communication has been established it will be easy to create an alphabet that will make it possible to converse with them.' So said the German geometer, but his plan was not carried out, and so far there has never been a direct link between the earth and its satellite. The feat of creating such a link has been reserved for the practical genius of the American people. The means of accomplishing it is simple, easy, and certain, and it is the subject of the proposal I am about to make to you."

There was a hubbub, a storm of exclamations. Every member of the audience was captivated and carried away by what Barbicane was saying.

"Listen! Silence!" they shouted from all over the hall.

When the agitation had died down, Barbicane resumed his interrupted speech in a deeper voice:

"You know the progress ballistics has made in recent

years, and how much more greatly firearms would have been perfected if the war had continued. You also know that, practically speaking, the strength of cannons and the expansive power of gunpowder are unlimited. Taking the fact as my starting point, I began to wonder whether, with a sufficiently large cannon, constructed in such a way as to assure the necessary resistance, it might not be possible to shoot a projectile to the moon."

An "Oh!" of stupefaction burst from a thousand gasping breasts; then there was a moment of silence like the deep calm that precedes a thunderstorm. And there was indeed thunder, but it was a thunder of applause and shouts that shook the hall. Barbicane tried to speak; in vain. Ten minutes went by before he was again able to make himself heard.

"Let me finish," he said calmly. "I have approached the problem with determination and considered it from every possible angle. From my incontestable calculations I have reached the conclusion that a correctly aimed projectile with an initial velocity of 36,000 feet per second is sure to reach the moon. And so, worthy colleagues, I respectfully propose that we undertake that little experiment!"

CHAPTER 3

THE EFFECT OF BARBICANE'S ANNOUNCEMENT

IT WOULD be impossible to depict the effect produced by these last words. What an uproar! What shouts of "Hurrah!" and "Hip, hip, hurray!" and all the other enthusiastic cheers that are so abundant in the American language! The disorder and commotion were indescribable. Mouths yelled, hands clapped, feet shook the floors of all the rooms. If all the cannons in that artillery museum had been fired at once, the din would not have been more violent. This is not surprising. There are gunners who are almost as noisy as their guns.

Barbicane remained calm in the midst of this wild acclaim. Perhaps he wanted to say a few more words to his colleagues, for his gestures demanded silence and his detonating bell exploded again and again. No one even heard it. He was soon lifted from his seat and carried off in triumph, and then from the hands of his faithful comrades he passed into the arms of an equally excited crowd.

Nothing can astonish an American. The French have often said that "the word 'impossible' is not French," but they have obviously been referring to the wrong language. In America, everything is easy, everything is simple, and mechanical difficulties are dead before they are born. No true Yankee would have allowed himself to see even the shadow of a difficulty between Barbicane's plan and its realization. No sooner said than done.

Barbicane's triumphal march continued into the night. It was a veritable torchlight parade. Irishmen, Germans, Frenchmen, Scotsmen, and all the other heterogeneous people who compose the population of Maryland shouted in their native languages. Hurrahs, vivats, and bravos were mingled in an ineffable burst of feeling.

Then, as though it had understood that all this tumult concerned it, the moon came out and began shining in serene splendor, eclipsing all the flames with its intense radiance. The Americans all looked up at its glowing disk. Some of them waved to it, some called it affectionate names, some sized it up, some shook their fists at it. Between eight o'clock and midnight an optician on Jones Street made a fortune selling telescopes. The crowd stared at the moon through telescopes as though they were staring at a great lady through opera glasses. They treated it casually as if they owned it. It seemed that blonde Phoebe belonged to those bold conquerors and was already part of the territory of the Union. And yet they were planning only to send a projectile to the moon. This is a rather brusque way of establishing relations, even with a satellite, but it is in very common use by civilized nations.

Even at midnight the general enthusiasm had still not begun to wane. It was maintained at an equal level in all classes of the population: politicians, scientists, businessmen, shopkeepers, laborers, intelligent people, and simpletons all felt stirred to their innermost depths. This was to be a national undertaking, so all parts of the city, and even the ships imprisoned in their basins, were overflowing with crowds drunk with joy, gin, and whiskey.

Everyone was conversing, holding forth, discussing, arguing, approving, and applauding, from the gentlemen lolling on the soft benches of barrooms with mugs of sherry cobbler,* to the boatmen getting drunk on knock-me-downs** in the dark taverns of Fell's Point.

Toward two o'clock in the morning the excitement finally died down. Barbicane succeeded in getting home, bruised, battered, and exhausted. Hercules himself would not have been able to withstand such enthusiasm. The crowd gradually deserted the streets and parks. The four railroads that converge at Baltimore scattered the multitude to the four corners of the United States and the city settled down to relative calm.

It should not be thought that Baltimore was the only city in the grip of such agitation during that memorable evening. The great cities of the Union—New York, Boston, Albany, Washington, Richmond, New Orleans, Charleston, Mobile—from Texas to Massachusetts, from Michigan to Florida, all shared in the delirium. The thirty thousand corresponding members of the Gun Club had seen their president's letter, and they had been waiting with equal impatience for the famous announcement of October 5. Thus that same evening, as the words came from Barbicane's lips they were transmitted all over the country on telegraph wires at a speed of 248,447 miles a second. It can therefore be said with absolute certainty that at the same moment the United States of America, ten times as big as France, shouted a single "Hurrah!" and that twenty-five million hearts, swelling with pride, beat with the same pulsation.

---

*A mixture of rum, orange juice, sugar, cinnamon, and nutmeg. This yellowish liquid is drunk from mugs through glass straws.

**An appalling drink of the lower classes.

The next day, fifteen hundred daily, weekly, semi-monthly, and monthly newspapers took up the matter. They examined its physical, meteorological, economical, and moral aspects; they considered it from the viewpoint of civilization and political advantage. They wondered if the moon was a finished world, one that was no longer undergoing any change. Was it like the earth before its atmosphere had been formed? What was the appearance of the side that could not be seen from the earth? Although sending a projectile to the moon was all that had been planned so far, every newspaper saw this as the beginning of a series of experiments. They all hoped that America would some day penetrate the last secrets of the mysterious lunar world, and some of them even seemed to fear that its conquest might upset the balance of power in Europe.

Once the plan had been discussed, not one publication expressed the slightest doubt that it would be carried out. Its advantages were pointed out by the reviews, pamphlets, bulletins, and magazines published by scientific, literary, and religious societies. The Natural History Society of Boston, the American Society of Science and Art of Albany, the Geographical and Statistical Society of New York, the American Philosophical Society of Philadelphia, and the Smithsonian Institution of Washington sent countless letters of congratulation to the Gun Club, with offers of service and money.

Thus it can be said that no other proposal ever attracted so many supporters. Hesitations, doubts, and misgivings were out of the question. As for the jokes, caricatures, and songs which, in Europe and especially in France, would have greeted the idea of sending a projectile to the moon, they would have been very dangerous to anyone rash enough to originate them: all the "lifepreservers"* in the world would have been powerless to save him from the general indignation. There are some things one does not laugh at in the New World. And so from that day onward Barbicane was one of the great citizens of the United States, something like the Washington of science. One incident, among others, will show the strength of this sudden devotion of an entire nation to one man.

Several days after the momentous meeting of the Gun Club, the director of a traveling English theatrical company announced that he was going to present Shakespeare's *Much Ado About Nothing* in a Baltimore theater. The population of the city saw the title as an offensive reference to Barbicane's plan. They rushed into the theater, broke up the seats, and forced the unfortunate director to change his program. The director was a clever man; bowing to public demand, he replaced the ill-chosen comedy with *As You Like It* and played to packed houses for many weeks.

---

*A pocket weapon made of flexible whalebone and a metal ball.

CHAPTER 4

REPLY FROM THE CAMBRIDGE
OBSERVATORY

MEANWHILE, AMID all the acclaim that was being given him, Barbicane was not wasting time. The first thing he did was to assemble his colleagues in the offices of the Gun Club. There, after discussing the matter, they agreed to consult some astronomers on the astronomical aspects of the project; then, when the reply had been received, they would consider the mechanical means, and nothing would be neglected in assuring the success of the great experiment.

A letter containing a number of precisely worded questions was sent to the observatory at Cambridge, Massachusetts. This city, where the first university in the United States was founded, is justly famous for its observatory. The staff attached to it is composed of scientists of the greatest merit; its powerful telescope is the one that enabled Bond to resolve the nebula of Andromeda, and Clarke to discover the satellite of Sirius. The Gun Club's confidence in this renowned establishment was therefore fully justified.

Two days later, the impatiently awaited reply was delivered to Barbicane:

Cambridge, October 7

> *Mr. Impey Barbicane*
> *President of the Gun Club*
> *Baltimore, Maryland*

Dear Mr. Barbicane,

On receipt of your letter of October 6, addressed to the Cambridge Observatory in the name of the Gun Club, our staff met immediately and drew up the following reply.

Your questions were these:

1. *Is it possible to send a projectile to the moon?*
2. *What is the exact distance between the earth and the moon?*
3. *If a projectile is given sufficient initial velocity, how long will it be in flight, and when must it be launched in order for it to strike the moon at a given point?*
4. *At what precise time is the moon in the most favorable position for being reached by the projectile?*
5. *At what point in the sky must the cannon that will launch the projectile be aimed?*
6. *What will be the position of the moon when the projectile is launched?*

Concerning the first question: Is it possible to send a projectile to the moon?

Yes, it is possible to do so, if the projectile is given an initial velocity of 36,000 feet per second. Calculation shows that this velocity is sufficient. As one moves away from the earth, the force of gravity diminishes in inverse ratio to the square of the distance; that is, for a distance three times as great, the force is nine times as small. Therefore, the weight of the projectile will decrease rapidly and will finally be reduced to zero when the gravitational pull of the moon balances that of the earth, which will occur when forty-seven fifty-seconds of the total distance has been covered. If it goes beyond that point, the projectile will be drawn to the moon by lunar gravity alone. The theoretical possibility of the feat is established beyond question; its actual accomplishment will depend solely on the power of the cannon employed.

Concerning the second question: What is the exact distance between the earth and the moon?

The moon does not describe a circle around the earth but an ellipse, one of whose foci is occupied by the earth. The moon is thus nearer to the earth at some times than at others, or, in astronomical terms, it is sometimes at its apogee and sometimes at its perigee. The difference between the two distances is not negligible. At its apogee the moon is 247,552 miles from the earth, and at its perigee it is 218,657 miles away, making a difference of 28,895 miles, or a ninth of the total distance. Calculations should therefore be based on the distance to the moon at its perigee.

Concerning the third question: If a projectile is given sufficient initial velocity, how long will it be in flight, and when must it be launched in order for it to strike the moon at a given point?

If the projectile kept its initial velocity of 36,000 feet per second, it would take only about nine hours to reach its destination; but its velocity will be constantly diminishing, and calculation shows that it will take 300,000 seconds, or eighty-three hours and twenty minutes, to reach the point where the earth's gravity is balanced by the moon's, and from this point it will fall to the moon in 50,000 seconds, or thirteen hours, fifty-three minutes, and twenty seconds. It should therefore be launched ninety-seven hours, thirteen minutes, and twenty seconds before the moon arrives at the point of aim.

Concerning the fourth question: At what precise time is the moon in the most favorable position for being reached by the projectile?

As has been said above, the projectile should be launched when the moon is at its perigee. Furthermore, it should be launched when the moon is at the zenith.* This will diminish the distance by the length of the earth's radius, i.e., 3,919 miles, so that the actual distance to be covered will be 214,973 miles. But while the moon reaches its perigee each month, it is not always at the zenith when it does so. These two conditions coincide only at long intervals. The projectile should not be launched until they do. Fortunately this will be the case on December 4 of next year: at midnight the moon will be at its perigee, i.e., at its shortest distance from the earth, and at the same time it will reach the zenith.

Concerning the fifth question: At what point in the sky must the cannon that will launch the projectile be aimed?

From the foregoing it is clear that the cannon must be aimed at the zenith, so that the line of fire

---

*The zenith is the point in the sky directly above the observer.

will be perpendicular to the plane of the horizon, and the projectile will escape from the earth's gravity more rapidly. But in order for the moon to rise to the zenith of a given place the latitude of the place must be no greater than the moon's declination; that is, the place must lie somewhere between the equator and the twenty-eighth parallel, either north or south.* At any other point, the line of fire would have to be oblique, and that would be detrimental to the success of the undertaking.

Concerning the sixth question: What will be the position of the moon when the projectile is launched?

When the projectile is launched, the moon, which advances thirteen degrees, ten minutes, and thirty-five seconds each day, will have to be four times that far from the zenith, or fifty-two degrees, forty-two minutes, and twenty seconds. This represents the distance it will cover during the flight of the projectile. But since the deviation imparted to the projectile by the rotation of the earth must also be taken into account, and since the projectile will not reach the moon until after it has deviated a distance equal to sixteen times the radius of the earth, which is equivalent to eleven degrees of the moon's orbit, these eleven degrees must be added to the fifty-two degrees mentioned above. Thus when the projectile is launched, the moon will be at an angle of approximately sixty-four degrees from the vertical.

Such are the answers to the questions asked of

---

*Only between the equator and the twenty-eighth parallel does the moon reach the zenith at its culmination. Beyond the twenty-eighth parallel, it approaches the zenith less and less as one moves toward the pole.

the Cambridge Observatory by the members of the Gun Club.

    To sum up:

1. *The cannon must be located no more than twenty-eight degrees from the equator.*
2. *It must be aimed at the zenith.*
3. *The projectile must be given an initial velocity of 36,000 feet per second.*
4. *It must be launched on December 1 of next year, at thirteen minutes and twenty seconds before eleven o'clock at night.*
5. *It will strike the moon four days after its departure, on December 4 at exactly midnight, just as the moon reaches the zenith.*

    The members of the Gun Club must therefore begin work without delay and be ready to launch their projectile at the right time, for if they miss the date of December 4 they will not find the moon in the same conditions of perigee and zenith until eighteen years and eleven days later.

    The staff of the Cambridge Observatory is entirely at your disposal for questions of theoretical astronomy, and joins its congratulations to those of all America.

Sincerely,
J. M. Belfast
Director

CHAPTER 5

THE ROMANCE OF THE MOON

AN OBSERVER endowed with infinitely penetrating vision, and placed at the unknown center around which the world gravitates, would have seen myriads of atoms filling space during the chaotic period of the universe. But gradually, as the centuries passed, a change took place; a law of attraction manifested itself and was obeyed by the atoms that had hitherto been wandering; they combined chemically, according to their affinities, grouped themselves into molecules and formed those nebulous masses which are strewn throughout the depths of space.

Each one of these masses soon acquired a movement of rotation around its central point. This center, composed of sparse molecules, began spinning and progressively condensing. In accordance with the immutable laws of mechanics, as its volume was diminished by condensation, its rotary motion was accelerated. From the continuation of these two effects there resulted a principal star, the center of the nebulous mass.

If he had watched attentively, the observer would then have seen other molecules in the mass behaving like the central star: condensing in a constantly accelerating rotary motion as it had done, and gravitating around it in the form of countless stars. A nebula had been formed. Astronomers now count nearly five thousand of them.

Among these five thousand nebulae there is one which men have named the Milky Way. It contains eighteen million stars, each one of which has become the center of a solar world.

If the observer had particularly examined one of the smallest* and brightest of those eighteen million stars, the one we proudly call the sun, all the phenomena to which the formation of the universe is due would have taken place before his eyes.

He would have seen the sun, still in a gaseous state and composed of loose molecules, turning on its axis to complete its work of concentration. This motion, faithful to the laws of mechanics, accelerated as the sun's volume decreased, and finally the time came when centrifugal force prevailed over centripetal force, which tends to push molecules toward the center.

Then another phenomenon would have taken place before the observer's eyes. Molecules located in the plane of the equator, escaping like a stone from a sling whose cord has just snapped, formed several concentric rings around the sun, like those of Saturn. These rings of cosmic matter rotated around the central mass, then began disintegrating and breaking up into secondary masses, i.e., into planets.

If the observer had watched these planets he would have seen them acting exactly like the sun and giving birth to one or more cosmic rings. This was the origin of those minor bodies known as satellites.

Thus, in going from the atom to the molecule, from the

---

*According to Wallaston, the diameter of Sirius must be twelve times that of the sun, or over ten million miles.

molecule to the nebulous mass, from the nebulous mass to the nebula, from the nebula to the principal star, from the principal star to the sun, from the sun to the planet, and from the planet to the satellite, we have the whole series of transformations undergone by heavenly bodies since the first days of the world.

The sun seems lost in the immensities of the stellar world, and yet current scientific theory tells us that it is part of the Milky Way. It is the center of a world, and, however small it may seem in the vast reaches of space, it is actually enormous, for its size is 1,400,000 times greater than that of the earth. Around it gravitate the eight planets that came from its entrails at the beginning of creation. In order of nearness to the sun, they are: Mercury, Venus, Earth, Mars, Jupiter, Saturn, Uranus, and Neptune. In addition, moving in regular orbits between Mars and Jupiter, there are smaller bodies which may be the debris of a larger body broken into thousands of pieces. The telescope has revealed ninety-seven of them so far.*

Some of these attendants of the sun, held in their elliptical orbits by the great law of gravitation, have their own satellites. Uranus and Saturn have eight each, Jupiter has four, Neptune may have three, the earth has one. The latter, one of the smallest in the solar system, is called the moon, and it was the objective that the bold American spirit had set out to conquer.

Because of its relative nearness and the rapidly changing spectacle of its various phases, the moon shared man's attention with the sun from the very beginning. But

*Some of these asteroids are so small that a man could run all the way around them in one day.

the sun is tiring to the eyes, and the splendor of its light soon forces those who look at it to avert their gaze.

Pale Phoebe, however, is more humane; she graciously lets herself be seen in all her modest charm; she is unassuming and gentle to the eye, and yet she sometimes takes the liberty of eclipsing her brother, the radiant Apollo, without ever being eclipsed by him. Realizing the debt of gratitude they owed to this faithful friend of the earth, the Mohammedans established their month in accordance with her revolution.*

The ancient nations worshiped that chaste goddess. The Egyptians called her Isis, the Phoenicians Astarte; the Greeks worshiped her under the name of Phoebe, daughter of Leto and Zeus, and they explained her eclipses by her mysterious visits to the handsome Endymion. Mythology tells us that the Nemean lion roamed the moon before appearing on earth, and the poet Agesianax, quoted by Plutarch, celebrated in his verses the gentle eyes, charming nose, and gracious mouth formed by the bright parts of the adorable Selene.

Although the ancients had a good understanding of the character, temperament, and general moral qualities of the moon from a mythological point of view, even the most learned of them were extremely ignorant of its physical nature.

Some ancient astronomers, however, discovered certain things about the moon that have been confirmed by modern science. While the Arcadians claimed to have lived on the earth at a time when the moon did not yet exist, while Tatius regarded it as a fragment of the sun, while Aristotle's disciple Clearchus held it to be a smooth mirror in which images of the ocean were reflected, and

*Approximately twenty-nine and a half days.

while others saw it only as a mass of vapor given off by the earth or a revolving globe that was half fire and half ice, a few learned men, by means of shrewd observations, lacking optical instruments, surmised most of the laws that govern it.

Thus Thales of Miletus, five hundred years before the birth of Christ, voiced the opinion that the moon was illuminated by the sun. Aristarchus of Samos gave the correct explanation of its phases. Cleomedes taught that it shone with reflected light. The Chaldean Berosus discovered that the duration of its rotation was equal to that of its revolution, and in this way he was able to explain the fact that it always presents the same side to the earth. Finally Hipparchus, nearly two centuries before Christ, recognized certain irregularities in its apparent motions.

These various observations were later confirmed, and were beneficial to later astronomers. Ptolemy in the second century, and the Arab Abul Wefa in the tenth, completed Hipparchus' discoveries concerning the irregularities of the moon's motion as it describes the undulating line of its orbit under the influence of the sun. Then Copernicus in the fifteenth century, and Tycho Brahe in the sixteenth, completely described the solar system and the part played by the moon in the assemblage of heavenly bodies.

At that time its motions were determined more or less accurately, but little was known of its physical constitution. Then Galileo explained the light phenomena that occurred at certain phases of the moon by the existence of mountains on its surface. He placed their average height at 27,000 feet.

Hevelius, a Danzig astronomer, later lowered the greatest heights to 15,600 feet, but his colleague Riccioli brought thcm up to 42,000.

At the end of the eighteenth century, Herschel, armed with a powerful telescope, drastically reduced the previous measurements. He gave 11,400 feet to the highest mountains and brought the average to only 2,400. But he, too, was mistaken. It took the observations of Schroeter, Louville, Halley, Nasmyth, Bianchini, Pastorf, Lohrmann, and Gruithuysen, and especially the patient studies of Beer and Moedeler, to settle the matter definitively. Thanks to these scientists, the height of the mountains of the moon is now perfectly known. Beer and Moedeler measured 1,905 mountains, of which six are greater than 15,600 in height, and twenty-two are higher than 14,400 feet.* The tallest peak rises 22,806 feet above the surface of the moon.

At the same time, visual exploration of the moon was being completed. It was seen to be riddled with craters, and its essentially volcanic nature became increasingly apparent with each observation. From the absence of refraction in the light from planets occulted by it, the conclusion was drawn that it must have almost no atmosphere. This lack of atmosphere implied a lack of water. It was therefore obvious that, to live under such conditions, the lunar inhabitants must have a special constitution and be radically different from the inhabitants of the earth.

Finally, thanks to new methods, improved instruments constantly scanned the moon, leaving no part of its visible surface unexplored, even though its diameter is 2,150 miles, about a quarter of the earth's, its area is one-thirteenth that of the earth, and its volume one-forty-ninth. None of these secrets could escape the eyes of the

---

*The height of Mont Blanc is 15,787 feet above sea level.

astronomers, and the skilled scientists carried their prodigious observations still further.

Thus they noticed that when the moon was full there were white lines across it, and black lines during its phases. They studied these lines with greater precision and succeeded in determining their nature. They were long, narrow furrows with parallel edges, usually ending in the vicinity of a crater, about fifty feet wide and anywhere from ten to a hundred miles long. The astronomers called them "grooves," but giving them that name was all they could do. As for the question of whether or not these grooves were the dry beds of former streams, they could not answer it satisfactorily. The Americans hoped to be able to solve this geological puzzle some day. They also intended to reconnoiter that series of parallel ramparts discovered on the surface of the moon by Gruithuysen, a learned Munich professor, who regarded them as a system of fortifications erected by lunar engineers. These two obscure points, and no doubt many others, could not be definitely settled until there had been direct communication with the moon.

There was nothing more to be known with regard to the intensity of its light: the scientists knew that it is three hundred thousand times weaker than that of the sun, and that its heat has no appreciable effect on a thermometer. As for the phenomenon known as "ashy light," it is explained by the effect of sunlight reflected from the earth to the moon, which seems to complete the lunar disk when it is seen in the shape of a crescent during its first and last phases.

Such was the state of acquired knowledge concerning the earth's satellite. The Gun Club proposed to augment it from every point of view: cosmographic, geological, political, and moral.

CHAPTER 6

WHAT IT IS IMPOSSIBLE NOT TO KNOW AND WHAT IT IS NO LONGER PERMISSIBLE TO BELIEVE IN THE UNITED STATES

ONE IMMEDIATE effect of Barbicane's proposal was to focus attention on all astronomical facts relating to the moon. Everyone had been studying it assiduously. It seemed that the moon had appeared on the horizon for the first time, that no one had ever seen it in the sky before. It became fashionable; it was the celebrity of the day without seeming less modest, and took its place among the "stars" without showing any more pride. The newspapers revived old stories in which the "wolves' sun" played a part; they recalled the influence that the ignorance of earlier times had attributed to it, they sang its praises in every way; they stopped just short of quoting its witty remarks. The whole country had a case of "moon fever."

The scientific journals dealt more specifically with matters concerning the Gun Club's project. They published the letter from the Cambridge Observatory, commented on it, and gave it their unqualified approval.

In short, it was no longer permissible for even the least learned American to be ignorant of a single one of the known facts about the moon, or for even the most narrow-minded old woman to go on entertaining superstitious beliefs about it. Science came to them in every form and penetrated through their eyes and ears. It was no longer possible to be an ignoramus—in astronomy.

Till then, many people did not know how the distance from the earth to the moon had been measured. Experts took the opportunity to tell them that it had been measured by means of the moon's parallax. If the word "parallax" seemed to surprise them, they were told that it was the angle formed by two straight lines projected to the moon from opposite ends of the earth's radius. If they doubted the accuracy of this method, it was immediately proven to them that not only was this average distance 234,347 miles, but that the astronomers' error was less than seventy miles.

For the sake of those who were not familiar with the motions of the moon, the newspapers demonstrated daily that it has two distinct motions—rotation on its axis and revolution around the earth—which both take place in the same length of time: twenty-seven and a third days.*

The movement of rotation is the one that makes day and night on the moon's surface; but there is only one day and one night per lunar month, and each lasts 354⅓ hours. Fortunately, however, the side turned toward the earth is illuminated by it with an intensity equal to the light of fourteen moons. As for the other side, which is always invisible to us, it naturally has 354⅓ hours of profound darkness mitigated only by "the pale glow that falls from the stars." This is due solely to the fact that the motions of rotation and revolution take place in exactly the same span of time, a phenomenon which, according to Cassini

*This is the duration of the sidereal revolution, i.e., the time it takes the moon to return to a given star.

and Herschel, is common to the satellites of Jupiter, and probably to all other satellites as well.

There were some well-meaning but rather dense people who at first could not understand that the same side of the moon is always visible from the earth because the moon rotates once on its axis during the time required for it to circle the earth. They were told, "Go into your dining room and walk around the table so that you're always looking at the center of it. When you've gone all the way around it, you'll have pivoted once on your own axis, too, because your eyes will have swept past every point in the room. The room is the sky, the table is the earth, and you're the moon!" And they were delighted with the comparison.

Thus the moon constantly shows the same side to the earth. To be precise, however, it must be added that as the result of a certain oscillation known as libration, we are able to see a little more than half of its surface: about fifty-seven percent of it.

When the ignorant had come to know as much as the director of the Cambridge Observatory about the moon's rotation, they became concerned with its revolution around the earth. A score of scientific journals quickly set about enlightening them. They learned that the firmament, with its infinity of stars, can be regarded as a vast dial on which the moon moves, indicating the correct time to the inhabitants of the earth; that it is in this movement that the moon shows its different phases; that the moon is full when it is in opposition to the sun, i.e., when the moon, earth, and sun form a straight line, with the earth in the middle; that the moon is new when it is in conjunction with the sun, i.e., when it is between it and the earth; and finally that the moon is in its first or last quarter when it forms a right angle with the sun and the earth, with itself at the vertex.

A few perspicacious Americans concluded from this that eclipses could take place only at times of conjunction or opposition, and their reasoning was sound. In conjunction, the moon can eclipse the sun, and in opposition the earth can eclipse the moon. These eclipses do not happen twice in a lunar month because the plane of the moon's motion is inclined to the ecliptic, that is, the plane of the earth's motion.

As for the height that the moon can reach above the horizon, the letter from the Cambridge Observatory had said everything on that subject. Everyone knew that this height varies according to the latitude of the place from which one is observing. But the only parts of the globe where the moon passes the zenith, that is, where it can be seen directly overhead, necessarily lie between the twenty-eighth parallels and the equator. Hence the important recommendation to perform the experiment in this part of the earth, so that the projectile could be launched perpendicularly and thus escape more quickly from the pull of gravity. It was an essential condition for the success of the enterprise, and public opinion was keenly interested in it.

As for the path followed by the moon in its revolution around the earth, the Cambridge Observatory had made it sufficiently clear, even to the most ignorant people in all countries, that this path is not a circle but an ellipse, with the earth occupying one of the foci. These elliptical orbits are common to all planets as well as all satellites, and rational mechanics proves conclusively that it could not be otherwise. It was widely understood that the moon is at its apogee when it is furthest from the earth, and at its perigee when it is nearest.

This, then, was what every American knew, whether he liked it or not, what no one could decently be ignorant of. But while these true principles were rapidly disseminated, it was less easy to uproot certain errors and illusory fears.

Some people maintained, for example, that the moon was a former comet which, while moving in its elongated orbit around the sun, had passed close to the earth and been captured by its gravity. These parlor astronomers felt that this explained the seared appearance of the moon, an irreparable misfortune for which they blamed the sun. But when it was pointed out to them that comets have an atmosphere, while the moon has either very little or none at all, they had nothing to say in reply.

Others, who belonged to the breed of tremblers, had certain fears with regard to the moon. They had heard that, since the observations made in days of the caliphs, its speed of revolution around the earth had been increasing. From this they concluded, quite logically, that the acceleration must indicate a decrease in the distance between the earth and the moon, and that if the process continued the moon would eventually fall against the earth. However, they had to be reassured and stop fearing for future generations when they were told that, according to the calculations of Laplace, a famous French mathematician, this acceleration is contained within very narrow limits, and that a proportionate diminution will soon follow. Thus the equilibrium of the solar system cannot be upset in the centuries to come.

In the last place came the superstitious category of the ignorant. These people are not content to lack knowledge: they claim to know things that are actually false, and they "knew" many such things about the moon. Some of them regarded it as a smooth mirror by means of which people could see each other from various points on the earth and communicate their thoughts. Others maintained that out of a thousand new moons that had been observed, nine hundred fifty had brought about notable changes such as cataclysms, revolutions, earthquakes, floods, etc. They thus believed that the moon had a mysterious influence on human destiny and considered it to be the "true counter-balance" of existence. They thought that each lunar inhabitant was attached to each inhabitant of the earth by a sympathetic bond. Following Dr. Mead they maintained that the vital system was completely dependent on the moon. They stubbornly insisted that boys were born mainly during the new moon and girls during the last quarter, etc., etc. But finally they had to give up these gross errors and return to the truth. Although the moon, stripped of all its influence, was diminished in the minds of those who paid court to all powers, and although some people turned their backs on it, the vast majority decided in favor of it. As for the Americans, their only ambition was now to take possession of that new continent in space, and plant the star-spangled banner of the United States on its highest peak.

CHAPTER 7

THE HYMN TO THE PROJECTILE

IN ITS memorable letter of October 7, the Cambridge Observatory had dealt with the problem from the astronomical point of view. It now had to be solved mechanically. At this point the practical difficulties would have been insurmountable in any other country than America. There, they were only child's play.

Without wasting any time, President Barbicane appointed an executive committee from among the members of the Gun Club. In three meetings this committee was to elucidate the three great questions of the cannon, the projectile, and the propellant. It was composed of four members who were highly learned in these matters: Barbicane, who had a deciding vote in case of deadlock, General Morgan, Major Elphiston, and finally the inevitable J. T. Maston, who was assigned to act as secretary and recorder.

On October 8 the committee met in Barbicane's house at 3 Republican Street. Since it was important that such a serious discussion should not be disturbed by the cries of the stomach, the four members of the Gun Club sat down around a table covered with sandwiches and large teapots. J. T. Maston screwed his pen into his iron hook and the meeting began.

Barbicane was the first to speak:

"Gentlemen, we must solve one of the most important problems of ballistics, that exalted science which deals with the motion of projectiles, or bodies launched into space by some sort of propelling power, then abandoned to themselves."

"Ah, ballistics!" J. T. Maston exclaimed with deep emotion.

"It might have seemed more logical," Barbicane went on, "to devote this first meeting to a discussion of the cannon . . ."

"Yes," remarked General Morgan.

"However," said Barbicane, "after thorough consideration it seems to me that the question of the projectile ought to take precedence over that of the cannon, and that the dimensions of the latter ought to depend on those of the former."

"I request permission to speak," said J. T. Maston.

It was granted to him with all due deference to his magnificent past.

"Valiant friends," he said in an inspired tone, "our president is right to give priority to the question of the projectile. The projectile we're going to send to the moon will be our messenger, our ambassador, and I would like to consider it from a purely moral point of view."

This new way of regarding a projectile aroused the curiosity of the other committee members. They listened to J. T. Maston with keen attention.

"My dear colleagues," he went on, "I'll be brief. I'll disregard the physical projectile, the one that kills, and consider only the mathematical, moral projectile. To me, the artillery projectile is the most brilliant manifestation of human power, which is entirely summed up in it. It was in creating it that man came closest to the Creator!"

"Well said!" exclaimed Major Elphiston.

"Yes," the orator continued, "God made the stars and the planets, but man made the artillery projectile, that criterion of earthly velocities, that miniature version of the heavenly bodies wandering in space—and they, after all, are only a different kind of projectile! To God belong the speeds of electricity, light, stars, comets, planets, satellites, sound, and wind, but to us belongs the speed of the artillery projectile, a hundred times greater than the speed of the fastest trains and horses!"

J. T. Maston was transported; his voice took on lyrical inflections as he sang this sacred hymn to the projectile.

"Would you like figures? I'll give you some eloquent ones! Let's consider only the modest twenty-four-pounder. It's true that it moves 800,000 times slower than electricity, 640,000 times slower than light, seventy-three times slower than the earth in its orbit around the sun, but when it leaves the cannon its speed is greater than that of sound:* it is traveling at the rate of 1,200 feet per second, 12,000 feet in ten seconds, 14 miles a minute, 840 miles an hour, 20,100 miles a day—approximately the same speed as a point on the equator in the earth's rotation—and 7,336,500 miles a year. At this speed it would take eleven days to reach the moon, twelve years to reach the sun, and 360 years to reach Neptune, at the outermost limit of the solar system. That's what that modest projectile, the work of our hands, could do! Just think what it will be like when we fire a projectile more than twenty times as fast, at a speed of seven miles a second! Ah, magnificent projectile, I like to think that you'll be received up there with all the honor befitting an ambassador of the earth!"

---

*Thus, if one has heard the sound of a cannon shot, one can no longer be struck by the projectile.

The end of this lofty speech was greeted with loud cheers, and J. T. Maston, overcome with emotion, sat down amid the congratulations of his colleagues.

"And now that we've paid ample tribute to poetry," said Barbicane, "let's approach the matter directly."

"We're ready," replied the committee as each man prepared to eat his sixth sandwich.

"You know the problem that must be solved," said Barbicane. "We must give a projectile a speed of 36,000 feet per second. I have reason to think we'll succeed. But now let's examine the speeds obtained so far. General Morgan can enlighten us on that subject."

"Yes, especially since I was on the Experiment Committee during the war," replied the general. "First, I can tell you that the Dahlgren hundred-pounders, which had a range of three miles, gave their projectiles a muzzle velocity of 1,500 feet per second."

"Good. And what about the Rodman Columbiad?"* asked Barbicane.

"The Rodman Columbiad, tested at Fort Hamilton, near New York City, shot a half-ton projectile six miles, with a muzzle velocity of 2,400 feet per second, a result never obtained by Armstrong and Paliser in England."

"Oh, the English!" said J. T. Maston, shaking his formidable hook at the horizon.

"So 2,400 feet per second is the highest velocity reached so far?" asked Barbicane.

"Yes," replied Morgan.

"I *will* say, however," remarked J. T. Maston, "that if my mortar hadn't burst..."

"Yes, but it did burst," Barbicane said with a benevo-

---

*This was the name given by the Americans to those enormous weapons of destruction.

lent gesture. "Now, let's take that velocity of 2,400 feet per second as our starting point. We'll have to increase it fifteenfold. I'll postpone discussing the means of achieving that velocity until another meeting! For the moment, I'd like to call your attention to the dimensions that the projectile will have to have. As you can well imagine, we won't be dealing with a little bullet weighing no more than half a ton!"

"Why not?" asked Major Elphiston.

"Because our projectile," J. T. Maston said quickly, "must be big enough to attract the attention of the inhabitants of the moon, if there are any."

"Yes," said Barbicane, "and also for an even more important reason."

"What do you mean?" asked the major.

"I mean that it's not enough to send off a projectile and then forget about it: we must be able to watch it until it reaches its destination."

"What!" exclaimed the general and the major, somewhat startled by this idea.

"If we can't watch it," Barbicane said with self-assurance, "our experiment will be inconclusive."

"Then you must be planning to make a projectile of colossal size!" said the major.

"No. Listen carefully. As you know, optical instruments have been highly developed. There are telescopes capable of magnifying objects six thousand times, and bringing the moon to an apparent distance of forty miles. At that distance, objects sixty feet wide are clearly visible. The reason why telescopes haven't been made any more powerful is that their clarity decreases as their power increases, and the moon, which is only a reflecting mirror, doesn't give off enough light to make it desirable to increase magnification beyond that point."

"Then what will you do?" asked the general. "Give your projectile a diameter of sixty feet?"

"No."

"Well, then, do you intend to make the moon brighter?"

"Yes, I do."

"You can't be serious!" cried J. T. Maston.

"It's really quite simple," said Barbicane. "If I succeed in diminishing the density of the atmosphere the moon's light travels through, haven't I, in effect, made its light brighter?"

"Of course."

"Very well: to obtain that result, all that's necessary is to place a telescope on a high mountain, and that's what we'll do."

"I surrender!" said the major. "You have a way of simplifying things . . . And what magnification do you expect to get that way?"

"Forty-eight thousand. That will bring the moon to within five miles, and objects only nine feet wide will be visible."

"Wonderful!" said J. T. Maston. "So our projectile will have a diameter of nine feet!"

"Exactly."

"Allow me to point out, however," said Major Elphiston, "that it will be so heavy that . . ."

"Before we discuss its weight, Major," said Barbicane, "let me tell you that our ancestors performed wonders in that domain. Far be it from me to say that the science of ballistics hasn't made progress, but we ought to realize that amazing results were obtained as long ago as the Middle Ages. I might even say that they were more amazing than ours."

"That's unbelievable!" said Morgan.

"Can you justify what you've said?" J. T. Maston asked sharply.

"Certainly," replied Barbicane. "I have examples to support it. During the siege of Constantinople by Mohammed II, in 1543, stone projectiles were used that weighed 1,900 pounds and must have had impressive dimensions."

"Ah," said the major, "1,900 pounds is a good weight!"

"At Malta, in the days of the knights, a cannon in Fort St. Elmo shot projectiles weighing 2,500 pounds."

"Incredible!"

"Finally, according to a French historian, in the reign of Louis XI a mortar shot a bombshell that weighed only five hundred pounds, but that bombshell went from the Bastille, a place where the insane imprisoned the sane, to Charenton, where the sane imprisoned the insane."

"Very good!" said J. T. Maston.

"Since then, what have we done, really? The Armstrong cannon shoots a five-hundred-pound ball, the Rodman Columbiad a projectile weighing half a ton. It seems that what projectiles have gained in range, they've lost in weight. If we turn our efforts in that direction, we should be able, with the progress of science, to make cannon balls ten times as heavy as those of Mohammed II and the Knights of Malta."

"That's obvious," said the major. "But what metal do you intend to use for our projectile?"

"Ordinary cast iron," said General Morgan.

"Cast iron?" J. T. Maston said scornfully. "That's too common for a projectile that's going to the moon!"

"Let's not exaggerate," said Morgan. "Cast iron will be good enough."

"Well, then," said Major Elphiston, "since its weight

will be proportional to its volume, a cast-iron ball nine feet in diameter will be fantastically heavy!"

"If it's solid, yes; but not if it's hollow," said Barbicane.

"Hollow! Is it going to be a shell, rather than a ball?"

"We can put messages in it," said J. T. Maston, "and samples of our production here on earth."

"Yes, it will be a shell," said Barbicane. "It must be; a nine-foot solid ball would weigh more than 200,000 pounds, and that's obviously much too heavy. However, since the projectile must have a certain stability, I propose to give it a weight of 20,000 pounds."

"How thick will its walls be?" asked the major.

"If we use standard proportions," said Morgan, "a nine-foot diameter will require walls at least two feet thick."

"That would be much too heavy," said Barbicane. "You must bear in mind that we're not designing a shell to pierce armor plate. Its walls need only be thick enough to withstand the pressure of the powder gases in the bore. So our problem is this: how thick must the walls of a cast-iron shell be if it's to weigh only 20,000 pounds? I'm sure our skilled calculator, Mr. Maston, can tell us that immediately."

"I'll be glad to," replied the honorable secretary of the committee.

He wrote a few algebraic formulas on a sheet of paper. Here and there he wrote a π or an x^2. He even appeared to extract a certain cube root with the greatest of ease. Finally he said:

"The walls could be no more than two inches thick."

"Would that be enough?" the major asked doubtfully.

"No, of course not," replied Barbicane.

"Then what shall we do?" the major asked with a puzzled look.

"We'll have to use some other metal than cast iron."

"Copper?"

"No, that's also too heavy. I have something better to suggest."

"What is it?"

"Aluminum," said Barbicane.

"Aluminum!" exclaimed his three colleagues.

"That's right, my friends. As you know, in 1854 a famous French chemist, Henri Sainte-Claire-Deville, succeeded in obtaining aluminum in a compact mass. That precious metal is as white as silver, as unchanging as gold, as tough as iron, as fusible as copper, and as light as glass. It's easily worked, it's extremely widespread in nature, since alumina forms the base of most rocks, it has only a third of the weight of iron, and it seems to have been created for the specific purpose of providing us with material for our projectile!"

"Hurrah for aluminum!" cried J. T. Maston, who was always very noisy in his moments of enthusiasm.

"But isn't aluminum very expensive to produce?" asked the major.

"It used to be," replied Barbicane. "When it was first discovered, it cost somewhere between $260 and $280 a pound, then it dropped to $27, and now it's down to $9."

"But $9 a pound," said the major, who did not give up easily, "is still an enormous price!"

"Enormous but not prohibitive."

"How much will the projectile weigh?" asked Morgan.

"Here are the results of my calculations," answered Barbicane. "A shell with a diameter of nine feet and walls a foot thick would weigh 67,440 pounds if it were made of cast iron. Made of aluminum, it will weigh only 19,250 pounds."

"Excellent!" said J. T. Maston. "That will fit into our project beautifully!"

"Excellent! Excellent!" repeated the major. "But do you realize that, at $9 a pound, the projectile will cost..."

"It will cost $173,250, yes, I'm aware of that; but don't worry, my friends: I assure you that our project won't be short of money."

"We'll be flooded with money!" said J. T. Maston.

"Well, what do you think of aluminum?" asked Barbicane.

"Motion carried!" replied the three other members of the committee.

"As for the shape of the shell," said Barbicane, "it's not important, because once the shell has gone through the earth's atmosphere it will be in a vacuum. So I propose a round ball; it can revolve if it wants to, and behave however it likes."

Thus ended the first meeting of the committee. The question of the projectile was settled, and J. T. Maston was delighted with the thought of sending an aluminum shell to the inhabitants of the moon: "It will give them an impressive idea of what we're like!"

CHAPTER 8

THE STORY OF THE CANNON

THE DECISIONS made at this meeting produced a great effect in the outside world. A few timorous people were alarmed by the idea of a 20,000-pound shell being shot into space. Everyone wondered what kind of a cannon would ever be able to give enough initial velocity to such a mass. These questions were to be triumphantly answered by the minutes of the committee's second meeting.

On the evening following the first meeting the four members of the committee sat down before new mountains of sandwiches and a veritable ocean of tea. The discussion was immediately resumed, this time without preliminaries.

"Gentlemen," said Barbicane, "we're now going to take up the question of the cannon that must be built: its length, shape, material, and weight. We'll probably give it gigantic dimensions, but no matter how great the difficulties, our industrial genius will easily overcome them. So please listen to me and don't hesitate to make blunt objections. I'm not afraid of them!"

This statement was greeted with a grunt of approval.

"Let me remind you," he went on, "where our discussion led us yesterday. We agreed that the problem is to give an initial velocity of 36,000 feet per second to a shell with a diameter of nine feet and a weight of 20,000 pounds."

"Yes, that's the problem," said Major Elphiston.

"I'll continue from there," said Barbicane. "When a projectile is launched into space, what happens? It's acted on by three independent forces: air resistance, the pull of the earth's gravity, and the propulsive force that's been applied to it. Let's examine these three forces. Air resistance will be unimportant. The earth's atmosphere is only forty miles thick. At a speed of 36,000 feet per second, the shell will go through it in five seconds, and that time is so short that we can regard air resistance as insignificant. Next, let's consider the pull of the earth's gravity, in other words the shell's weight. We know that its weight will diminish in inverse ratio to the square of its distance from the earth. Here's what physics tells us: when a body is dropped near the surface of the earth, it falls fifteen feet in the first second, but if it were as far away from the earth as the moon is—257,542 miles—it would fall only a twentieth of an inch in the first second; in short, it would remain almost motionless. So we must progressively conquer the force of gravity. How will we do it? By the propulsive force we'll use."

"That's the difficulty," said the major.

"Yes, it is, but we'll overcome it, because the propulsive force we need will result from the length of the cannon and the amount of powder used. This amount will be limited only by the strength of the cannon. We must now decide on the dimensions of the cannon. Practically speaking, we can make it as strong as we like, because it won't have to be moved."

"That's all obvious," said General Morgan.

"So far the longest cannons made, our enormous

Columbiads, have had a length of only twenty-five feet, so we're going to surprise many people by the size we'll have to adopt."

"I'm sure we will!" said J. T. Maston. "I think we ought to make our cannon at least half a mile long!"

"Half a mile!" exclaimed the major and the general.

"Yes, half a mile, and it still won't be half long enough."

"Come, come, Maston," said Morgan, "you're exaggerating."

"I am not!" retorted the fiery secretary. "I don't know how you can say a thing like that!"

"I said it because you're going too far."

"Sir," J. T. Maston said loftily, "you'd do well to remember that an artilleryman is like a cannon ball: he can never go too far!"

Barbicane intervened to prevent the discussion from becoming too personal:

"Be calm, my friends. Let's reason. Our cannon will obviously have to be long enough to take full advantage of the expanding gases behind the shell, but it would be useless to go beyond a certain limit."

"Naturally," said the major.

"What rules are followed in such cases? The length of a cannon is usually from twenty to twenty-five times the diameter of its projectile, and it weighs between 235 and 240 times as much."

"That's not enough!" J. T. Maston said impetuously.

"I agree. According to that rule, the cannon for a projectile with a diameter of nine feet and a weight of 20,000 pounds would be only 225 feet long and would weigh only 4,800,000 pounds."

"That's ridiculous!" said J. T. Maston. "We might as well use a pistol!"

"I think so too," said Barbicane, "and so I propose that we quadruple that length and make a cannon nine hundred feet long."

The general and the major raised a few objections, but the proposal, vigorously supported by J. T. Maston, was finally adopted.

"And now," said the major, "how thick shall we make the walls of the cannon?"

"Six feet," replied Barbicane.

"You're not thinking of putting a mass like that on a gun carriage, are you?" asked the major.

"It would be magnificent!" said J. T. Maston.

"But unfeasible," said Barbicane. "No, I'm thinking of casting the cannon in the ground, reinforcing it with wrought-iron bands, and surrounding it with masonry, so that it will benefit from the resistance of the earth around it. When the barrel has been cast, it will be carefully reamed and measured to avoid the slightest gap between the projectile and the bore. That way, there will be no loss of gas and all the expansive power of the gunpowder will be used for propulsion."

"Hurrah!" cried J. T. Maston. "We've got our cannon!"

"Not yet," said Barbicane, calming him with his hand.

"Why not?"

"Because we haven't discussed its shape. Will it be a cannon, a howitzer, or a mortar?"

"A cannon," said General Morgan.

"A howitzer," said Major Elphiston.

"A mortar!" said J. T. Maston.

Another argument was about to break out, with each of the three advocating his favorite weapon, when Barbicane cut it short:

"My friends, I'm going to put you all in agreement. Our Columbiad will be all three of those weapons at once. It will be a cannon, since its chamber will have the same diameter as its bore; it will be a howitzer, since it will fire a hollow shell; and it will be a mortar, since it will be elevated at an angle of ninety degrees, and since, set firmly in the earth with no possibility of recoil, it will transmit its full propulsive power to the projectile."

The three men voiced their approval.

"I'd like to ask one question," said the major. "Will this cannon-howitzer-mortar have a rifled bore?"

"No," replied Barbicane. "We'll need an enormous initial velocity, and, as you know, a smoothbore barrel fires a ball faster than a rifled one."

"That's true."

"*Now* we've got it!" said J. T. Maston.

"Not quite," said Barbicane.

"Why not?"

"Because we don't know what metal it will be made of."

"Let's decide right now."

"That's what I was about to suggest."

Each member of the committee downed a dozen sandwiches, followed by a large cup of tea, and the discussion was resumed.

"My friends," said Barbicane, "our cannon must be extremely tough and hard, infusible, rustproof, and impervious to the corrosive action of acids."

"There's no doubt about that," said the major, "and since we'll have to use a huge amount of metal, we won't have a very wide choice."

"I propose that we use the best alloy discovered so

far," said the general: "a hundred parts copper, twelve parts tin, and six parts brass."

"I admit that's an alloy which has given very good results," said Barbicane, "but in this case it would be too expensive and hard to use. I think we'll have to use a cheap but excellent metal such as cast iron. Don't you agree, Major?"

"Certainly."

"Cast iron costs only a tenth as much as bronze. It's easy to melt, it can be simply cast in sand molds, and it can be quickly worked, so it will save us time as well as money. Furthermore, it's quite good. I remember that during the siege of Atlanta there were cast-iron cannons that fired a thousand shots apiece, at the rate of one every twenty minutes, without suffering any damage."

"But cast iron is very brittle," said the general.

"And very strong, too. Our cannon won't burst, I guarantee you that."

"A burst barrel is no disgrace," J. T. Maston said sententiously.

"Of course not," replied Barbicane. "I'm now going to ask our worthy secretary to calculate the weight of a cast-iron cannon with a length of 900 feet, an inner diameter of nine feet, and walls of six feet thick."

"Just a moment," said J. T. Maston.

As he had done the day before, he wrote out his formulas with wondrous ease, and a minute later he announced:

"The cannon will weigh 68,040 tons."

"And at two cents a pound, how much will it cost?"

"It will cost $2,721,600."

J. T. Maston, the major, and the general looked at Barbicane with anxiety.

"Well, my friends," he said, "I'll repeat what I told

you yesterday: don't worry, we'll have no shortage of money!"

After this assurance from the president of the Gun Club, the meeting ended and the committee agreed to meet again the following evening.

CHAPTER 9

THE QUESTION OF POWDER

THE QUESTION of powder still had to be dealt with. The public was eagerly awaiting this final decision. Now that the respective sizes of the projectile and the cannon had been established, how much gunpowder would be needed to provide the necessary propulsion? That formidable substance, which man had succeeded in bringing under his control, would have to be used in unheard-of amounts.

It is generally known and often repeated that gunpowder was invented in the fourteenth century by a monk named Schwarz, who paid for his great discovery with his life. But it has now been almost certainly proven that this story must be classified as a medieval legend. Gunpowder was invented by no one. It is directly descended from "Greek fire," which, like it, is composed of sulfur and saltpeter; but in the course of time those deflagrating mixtures were transformed into explosive ones.

But while the learned are perfectly familiar with the false history of gunpowder, few people realize its mechanical power. This must be known in order to understand the importance of the question under consideration by the committee.

A quart of gunpowder weighs about two pounds. When it burns, it produces 400 quarts of gas. When this gas is released, under the effect of a temperature of 2,400 degrees, it occupies a volume of 4,000 quarts. Thus the ratio between a certain volume of gunpowder and the volume of gas it produces when it burns is 4,000 to one. It is not difficult to imagine the awesome power of that gas when it is confined in a space 4,000 times too small for it.

The members of the committee were well aware of this when they began their third meeting. Barbicane gave the floor to Major Elphiston, who had been in charge of powder production during the war.

"Gentlemen," said the distinguished chemist, "I'll begin by giving you some undeniable figures that we can use as a basis for discussion. The twenty-four-pounder, which our honorable secretary spoke about so poetically the day before yesterday, uses only sixteen pounds of powder to fire its ball."

"Are you sure of that figure?" asked Barbicane.

"Quite sure. The Armstrong cannon uses only seventy-five pounds of powder for its 800-pound projectile, and the Rodman Columbiad uses only 160 pounds of powder to shoot its half-ton projectile a distance of six miles. These facts are incontestable, because I personally gathered them from the reports of the Artillery Committee."

"That's perfectly true," said the general.

"Here's the conclusion to be drawn from these figures," said the major: "the quantity of powder doesn't increase in direct proportion to the weight of the projectile. The twenty-four-pounder uses sixteen pounds of powder, or two-thirds the weight of its projectile, but that ratio isn't constant.

"If it were, a projectile weighing half a ton would require 667 pounds of powder, but it actually requires only 160 pounds."

"What point are you trying to make?" asked Barbicane.

"If you carry your theory to its logical conclusion, Major," said J. T. Maston, "you'll have to maintain that when the projectile becomes heavy enough, it won't need any powder at all!"

"You're playful even in the midst of a serious discussion, Maston," said the major, "but don't worry: I'll soon propose a quantity of powder that will satisfy your honor as an artilleryman. I do want to point out, however, that after experiments made during the war the powder charge for the biggest cannons was reduced to a tenth of the weight of their projectiles."

"That's also perfectly true," said the general. "But before we decide on the amount of powder necessary to propel our projectile, I think we'd better agree on what kind of powder we'll use."

"We'll use coarse-grained powder," said the major. "It burns faster than fine-grained powder."

"Yes," said the general, "but it has a high degree of brisance and eventually damages a gun's bore."

"That's a drawback for a cannon meant for long use, but not for our Columbiad. We'll run no risk of a burst barrel, and the powder will have to ignite very quickly, so that its energy will be completely utilized."

"We could make several priming holes," said J. T. Maston, "and ignite the powder at different places simultaneously."

"I suppose so," replied the major, "but that would make the operation more difficult. I'll stick to my coarse-grained powder because it will eliminate such difficulties."

"So be it," said the general.

"In his Columbiad," said the major, "Rodman used a powder with grains the size of chestnuts, made of willow charcoal that was simply roasted in iron boilers. It was hard and glossy, left no trace on the hand, contained a high proportion of hydrogen and oxygen, burned instantaneously, and, despite its great brisance, it wasn't hard on gun barrels."

"Then I don't see any reason to hesitate," said J. T. Maston. "Our choice is clear."

"Unless you'd prefer gold powder," said the major, laughing. This earned him a threatening gesture from his touchy friend's iron hook.

So far Barbicane had remained aloof from the discussion. He had been merely listening and letting the others talk. It was obvious that he had an idea. He contented himself with saying:

"And now, my friends, what quantity of powder do you propose?"

His three colleagues looked at one another for a few moments. Finally the general said, "Two hundred thousand pounds."

"Five hundred thousand," said the major.

"Eight hundred thousand pounds!" said J. T. Maston.

This time the major could not accuse him of exaggerating. After all, they were planning to send a 20,000-pound projectile to the moon with an initial velocity of 36,000 feet per second. There was a silence after the three men had made their respective proposals.

It was finally broken by Barbicane:

"Gentlemen," he said calmly, "I start from the principle that the strength of our cannon, built correctly, will be unlimited. I'm therefore going to surprise Mr. Maston by proposing to double his 800,000 pounds of powder."

"A million six hundred thousand pounds?" said J. T. Maston, bounding on his chair.

"Yes."

"But then we'll have to come back to my half-mile cannon!"

"That's obvious," said the major.

"A million six hundred thousand pounds of powder," said J. T. Maston, "will occupy a volume of about 22,000 cubic feet. Since your cannon has a capacity of only 54,000 cubic feet, it will be half full, and the bore will be so short that the expanding gases won't be able to give the projectile enough velocity."

There was no answer to that. J. T. Maston had spoken the truth. They all looked at Barbicane.

"Nevertheless," he said, "I insist on using that much powder. Think of it: 1,600,000 pounds of powder will produce 2,500,000 cubic feet of gas. Two and a half million! Do you realize what that means?"

"But how can we do it?" asked the general.

"It's quite simple: we must reduce that enormous mass of powder without diminishing its power."

"Very well, but how?"

"I'll tell you," Barbicane said simply. The others stared at him eagerly. "Nothing could be simpler than to reduce that amount of powder to a quarter of its normal volume. You're all familiar with that singular substance which forms the elementary tissues of plants and is known as cellulose."

"Ah, now I understand you!" said the major.

"It can be obtained in a pure state from various sources," Barbicane went on, "especially cotton, which is the fiber that surrounds the seeds of the cotton plant. When cotton is combined with cold nitric acid, it's transformed into a substance that's extremely insoluble, combustible, and explosive. It was discovered over thirty years ago, in 1832, by a French chemist named

Braconnot. He called it *xyloïdine*. In 1838 another Frenchman, Pelouze, studied its various properties, and in 1846 Schönbein, a chemistry professor in Basel, proposed that it be used as gunpowder. That powder is known as guncotton."

"Or pyroxylin," said the major.

"Or nitrocellulose," said the general.

"Wasn't there at least one American involved in the discovery?" asked J. T. Maston, moved by a keen feeling of national pride.

"Not a single one, unfortunately," said the major.

"If it will make you feel better," said Barbicane, "I'll tell you that one American's work is important in the study of cellulose, because collodion, one of the main agents in photography, is simply pyroxylin dissolved in alcohol and ether, and it was discovered by Maynard, who was a medical student in Boston at the time."

"Hurrah for Maynard and pyroxylin!" cried the noisy secretary of the Gun Club.

"To return to guncotton," said Barbicane, "you all know the properties that will make it so valuable to us. It can be made very easily: you soak cotton in nitric acid for fifteen minutes, rinse it with water, let it dry, and that's all."

"What could be simpler?" said the general.

"Furthermore, guncotton is unaffected by humidity. That's a valuable quality for our purposes, since it will take several days to load the cannon. It ignites at 160 degrees centigrade instead of 240, and it burns so quickly that if it's placed on top of a charge of ordinary powder and ignited, the ordinary powder won't have time to catch fire."

"It sounds perfect," said the major.

"However, it's very expensive."

"What does that matter?" said J. T. Maston.

"Finally, it can fire a projectile four times faster than ordinary powder can. And if it's mixed with a quantity of potassium nitrate equal to eighty percent of its weight, its power is increased still more."

"Will that be necessary?" asked the major.

"I don't think so," replied Barbicane. "So instead of 1,600,000 pounds of powder, we'll have only 400,000 pounds of guncotton. Since 500 pounds of it can safely be compressed into a volume of twenty-seven cubic feet, the whole charge will take up only 180 feet of the cannon's length, and the 2,500,000 cubic feet of gas will drive the shell through more than 700 feet of bore before sending it on its way toward the moon."

At these eloquent words, J. T. Maston was unable to contain his emotion: he threw himself into his friend's arms with the force of a cannon ball, and would have knocked him flat if Barbicane had not been built to withstand the most violent bombardment.

This incident ended the third meeting of the committee. Barbicane and his daring colleagues, to whom nothing seemed impossible, had just settled the complex questions of the projectile, the cannon, and the powder. Their plan was decided upon; they now had only to carry it out.

"That's only a detail, a mere trifle," said J. T. Maston.

Note: In the course of the above discussion, Barbicane credits one of his compatriots with the invention of collodion. This is a mistake, with all due deference to J. T. Maston, and it has arisen from the similarity between two names.

It is true that in 1847 Maynard, then a Boston medical student, had the idea of using collodion in the treatment of wounds, but collodion was already known in 1846. The honor of that great discovery must go to a Frenchman, a distinguished mind, a chemist who is also a painter, a poet, a philosopher, and a Hellenist: M. Louis Ménard.

CHAPTER 10

ONE ENEMY AMONG TWENTY-FIVE MILLION FRIENDS

T HE AMERICAN public took great interest in every detail of the Gun Club's project. They followed the committee's discussions day by day. They were fascinated by the simplest preparations for the great experiment, the questions of figures that it raised, the mechanical difficulties that would have to be overcome—in short, the whole process of getting the operation under way.

More than a year was to pass between the beginning of the work and its completion, but that time would not be devoid of excitement. The site to be chosen for the hole in the ground, the construction of the mold, the casting of the cannon, its highly dangerous loading: these things were more than enough to arouse the public's curiosity. When the projectile was fired, it would be out of sight in a few tenths of a second; from then on, only a privileged few would be able to see what would become of it, how it would behave in space, and how it would reach the moon. For this reason, the main interest lay in the preparations for the experiment and the precise details of its execution.

But to its purely scientific interest was suddenly added the commotion stirred up by an incident.

We have already seen how many friends and admirers Barbicane's project had attracted to him. Honorable and extraordinary though it was, however, this majority was not unanimous. One man in all the states of the Union protested against the project. He attacked it violently at every opportunity, and human nature is so made that Barbicane was more strongly affected by that one man's opposition than he was by the applause of all the others.

Yet he well knew the motive of that antipathy, the source of that solitary enmity, why it was personal and of long standing, and the rancorous rivalry that had produced it.

He had never seen that determined enemy. This was fortunate, for an encounter between the two men would certainly have had regrettable consequences. That rival was a scientist like Barbicane, a proud, dauntless, earnest, violent man, a pure Yankee. His name was Captain Nicholl. He lived in Philadelphia.

Everyone knows of the strange struggle that took place during the Civil War between cannons and naval armor, with the former determined to pierce the latter, and the latter determined to withstand the former. It led to radical changes in the navies of both continents. Projectiles and armor plate fought relentlessly; the first constantly grew larger as the second grew thicker. Ships armed with formidable guns moved into battle beneath the protection of their invulnerable iron shells. Vessels such as the *Merrimac,* the *Monitor* and the *Weehawken* fired enormous projectiles after armoring themselves against those of the enemy. They did unto others as they would not have had others do unto them, an immoral principle on which the whole art of war is based.

Barbicane was a great caster of projectiles, and Nicholl was a great forger of armor. One cast night and day in Baltimore, while the other forged day and night in

Philadelphia. Each was pursuing a line of thought essentially opposed to that of the other.

As soon as Barbicane invented a new projectile, Nicholl invented a new armor plate. Barbicane spent all his time making holes, Nicholl in preventing him from doing so—hence a constant rivalry that soon became personal. Nicholl appeared in Barbicane's dreams as an impenetrable armor plate which he crashed into at high speed, and Barbicane appeared in Nicholl's dreams as a projectile that cut him in half.

Although they were following divergent lines, the two scientists would eventually have encountered each other, despite all the axioms of geometry—but it would have been on the field of honor. Fortunately for these citizens so useful to their country, they were separated by a distance of fifty or sixty miles, and their friends placed so many obstacles along the way that they never met.

It was not clear which of the two inventors had gotten the better of the other; the results obtained made it difficult to form a precise judgment. It seemed, however, that in the long run the armor plate would have to yield to the projectile.

Nevertheless there were competent men who had their doubts. In a recent test, Barbicane's cylindro-conical projectiles had stuck in Nicholl's armor like pins. Nicholl had considered himself victorious and displayed unbounded contempt for his rival. But when Barbicane later replaced his conical projectiles with ordinary 600-pound shells, the captain had to change his tune. Although they had only a moderate velocity,* these projectiles pierced, cracked, and shattered the best armor plate.

Things had reached this point, with victory apparently

---

*The weight of the powder used was only a twelfth of the weight of the shell.

won by the projectile, when the war ended on the very day that Nicholl finished his new forged steel armor! It was a masterpiece of its kind; it would defy all the projectiles in the world. Nicholl had it taken to the experimental range in Washington and challenged Barbicane to pierce it. But now that the war was over, Barbicane did not want to make the test.

Captain Nicholl, infuriated, offered to expose his armor to projectiles of every conceivable kind: solid, hollow, round, or conical. He met with another refusal from Barbicane, who was apparently determined not to jeopardize the victory he had won.

Thrown into a frenzy by this unspeakable obstinacy, Nicholl tried to tempt Barbicane by making the conditions as favorable for him as possible. He offered to put his armor only two hundred yards from the cannon. Barbicane maintained his stubborn refusal. A hundred yards? No, not even at seventy-five.

"Fifty yards, then!" Nicholl said through the medium of the newspapers. "Or I'm even willing to put my armor only twenty-five yards away, and I'll stand behind it!"

Barbicane answered that even if Captain Nicholl stood in front of it, he still would not shoot.

Nicholl could no longer restrain himself when he learned of this reply. He made some personal remarks. He said that cowardice was cowardice, no matter what form it took; that a man who refused to fire a cannon was very close to being afraid to do it; that the artillerymen who now fought at a distance of six miles had prudently replaced individual courage with mathematical formulas; and that, furthermore, it took as much bravery to wait calmly for a cannon ball behind a sheet of armor as it did to shoot one under all the proper conditions.

Barbicane made no reply to these insinuations; he may

not even have known about them, for he was then completely absorbed in making plans for his great undertaking.

When Barbicane made his famous speech to the Gun Club, Captain Nicholl's anger reached its peak. It was mingled with supreme jealousy and a feeling of absolute impotence. How could he possibly invent something better than that 900-foot cannon? What armor could ever withstand a 20,000-pound projectile? At first he was staggered, overwhelmed, stunned by that cruel blow. Then he recovered his strength and resolved to crush the project beneath the weight of his arguments. He violently attacked the work of the Gun Club. He wrote a number of letters which the newspapers did not refuse to print. He tried to demolish Barbicane's plans scientifically. Once he had declared war, he resorted to all kinds of arguments, and it must be said that all too often they were specious and ungentlemanly.

First, Barbicane was violently attacked in his figures; Nicholl tried to demonstrate by rigorous logic that his calculations were wrong, and he accused him of not knowing the elementary principles of ballistics. Among other things, he stated that it was absolutely impossible to give any object a speed of 36,000 feet per second, and he further maintained, algebra in hand, that even at that speed such a heavy projectile would never get beyond the earth's atmosphere. It would fall back before it reached a height of twenty miles! Furthermore, even assuming that the velocity could be attained, and that it would be sufficient, the shell would not withstand the pressure of the gas produced by the combustion of 1,600,000 pounds of powder, and even if it should withstand the pressure it would not resist the temperature: it would melt by the time it left the muzzle of the cannon, and would then fall in a hot, searing rain on the heads of the foolhardy on-lookers.

Barbicane ignored these attacks and went on with his work.

Nicholl took a different approach. Without consider-ing its uselessness from every point of view, he regarded the experiment as extremely dangerous, for the towns near the deplorable cannon as well as for the citizens who would authorize such a reprehensible spectacle by their presence. He also pointed out that if the projectile did not reach its goal, which it could not possibly do, it would necessarily fall back to earth, and that the impact of such a mass, multiplied by the square of the distance, would cause great damage to some point on the globe. For these reasons he felt that, with all due respect to the rights of free citizens, this was a case in which the intervention of the government was necessary, in order to prevent one man's whim from endangering large numbers of people.

Such were the extremes of exaggeration to which Captain Nicholl let himself be driven. His opinions were not shared by anyone, so no account was taken of his dire predictions. He was allowed to shout himself hoarse, since he apparently enjoyed it. He had made himself the defender of a cause that was lost in advance. He was heard but not listened to, and he did not take one single admirer away from Barbicane, who did not even bother to answer his rival's arguments.

Nicholl was desperate. Unable to risk his life for his cause, he decided to risk his money. He publicly an-nounced in the *Richmond Enquirer* that he was willing to make the following bets:

1. That the Gun Club could not obtain the funds necessary for its project $1,000

2. That the casting of a 900-foot cannon was unfeasible and would not succeed $2,000

3. That it would be impossible to load the cannon, and that the guncotton would be prematurely ignited by the pressure of the projectile........$3,000

4. That the cannon would burst the first time it was fired...$4,000

5. That the projectile would reach a height of less than six miles and would fall back to earth a few seconds after being fired............................$5,000

Thus, in his invincible obstinacy, Captain Nicholl was risking no less than $15,000!

Despite the greatness of the sum he had offered to bet, on October 19, he received a sealed envelope containing this haughtily laconic reply:

Baltimore, October 18

Bet accepted.

Barbicane

CHAPTER 11

FLORIDA AND TEXAS

MEANWHILE THERE was one matter that still had to be decided: a favorable place had to be chosen for the experiment. According to the recommendations of the Cambridge Observatory, the projectile would have to be fired perpendicular to the plane of the horizon, that is, toward the zenith. The moon rises to the zenith only in places located between zero and twenty-eight degrees of latitude; in other words, its declination* is only twenty-eight degrees. The Gun Club therefore had to determine the exact spot on the globe where the immense cannon would be cast.

On October 20, at a general meeting of the club, Barbicane brought a copy of Z. Belltrop's magnificent map of the United States. But before he could unfold it, J. T. Maston asked for the floor with his usual vehemence and began speaking as follows:

"Gentlemen, the matter we're going to deal with today is of truly national importance, and it will give us an opportunity to perform a great act of patriotism."

The members of the Gun Club looked at one another without understanding what he had in mind.

---

*The declination of a heavenly body is its latitude in the celestial sphere; its right ascension is its longitude.

"None of you," he went on, "would ever dream of compromising when the glory of our country is at stake, and if there's one right that the Union can claim, it's the right to have our formidable cannon within its boundaries. Now, under present circumstances..."

"Good old Maston..." said Barbicane.

"Let me finish my thoughts. Under present circumstances we're forced to choose a place fairly near the equator so that conditions will be right for our experiment..."

"Will you please..." said Barbicane.

"I demand free discussion of ideas," retorted the impetuous J. T. Maston, "and I maintain that the ground from which our glorious projectile will be launched must belong to the Union."

"Of course!" said several members.

"Well, then, since our borders aren't wide enough, since the ocean constitutes an insurmountable obstacle to the south, since we must seek that twenty-eighth parallel in a country adjacent to the United States, we have a legitimate reason for fighting, and I demand that we declare war on Mexico!"

"No! No!" cried the members from all over the room.

"No?" said J. T. Maston. "That's a word I thought I'd never hear within these walls!"

"But listen..."

"Never! Never!" shouted the fiery orator. "Sooner or later that war will be fought, and I demand that it be declared this very day!"

"Maston," said Barbicane, firing his detonating bell, "you no longer have the floor!"

Maston tried to make a rejoinder, but several of his colleagues succeeded in controlling him.

"I agree," said Barbicane, "that the experiment can and

must take place only on the territory of the Union, but if my impatient friend had let me speak, if he had glanced at a map, he would know that there's no need to declare war on our neighbors, because some borders of the United States are below the twenty-eighth parallel. As you can see from this map, we have the whole southern part of Texas and Florida at our disposal."

The incident was closed, but it was not without regret that J. T. Maston let himself be convinced. It was decided that the cannon would be cast in either Texas or Florida. But this decision was to stir up an unparalleled rivalry between the towns of those two states.

When it meets the American coast, the twenty-eighth parallel runs across the Florida peninsula and divides it into two almost equal parts. Then it plunges into the Gulf of Mexico, passes beneath the arc formed by the coasts of Alabama, Mississippi, and Louisiana, cuts off one corner of Texas, extends into Mexico, crosses Sonora and Baja California, and heads into the vast Pacific. And so only those portions of Texas and Florida below this parallel fulfilled the conditions of latitude recommended by the Cambridge Observatory.

Southern Florida has no sizable towns, only forts erected against wandering Indians. Tampa was the only town that could point to its location and put forward a claim to be chosen as the site of the experiment.

In Texas, however, the towns are larger and more numerous. Corpus Christi in Nuecas County, all the towns on the Rio Grande, such as Laredo, Comalites, and San Ignacio in Webb County, Roma and Rio Grande City in Starr County, Edinburg in Hidalgo County, and Santa Rita, El Panda, and Brownsville in Cameron County formed an imposing league against the claims of Florida.

Shortly after the decision was made known, delegates

from Texas and Florida arrived in Baltimore. From then on, Barbicane and the influential members of the Gun Club were besieged night and day by overwhelming assertions and demands. Seven Greek cities quarreled over the honor of having been Homer's birthplace, but two whole states now threatened to come to blows over a cannon.

These "fierce brothers" walked the streets of the city in armed groups. Each time they met there was danger of a conflict that would have had disastrous consequences. Fortunately Barbicane's caution and adroitness warded off this danger. Personal feelings were given an outlet in the newspapers of the various states. The *New York Herald* and the *Tribune,* for example, supported Texas, while the *Times* and the *American Review* took up the cause of Florida. The members of the Gun Club did not know which to listen to.

Texas proudly pointed to its twenty-six counties and seemed to line them up in battle array; Florida replied that its twelve counties could do more than twenty-six in a state that was six times bigger.

Texas bragged about its 330,000 inhabitants; Florida boasted that it was more densely populated with its 56,000 inhabitants, since its area was so much smaller. Furthermore, it accused Texas of specializing in malaria, which took the lives of several thousand people every year. And it was true.

Texas replied that Florida was second to none when it came to fevers, and that it was rash, to say the least, to accuse other places of being unhealthy when it had the honor of having *vomigo negro* in a chronic state. And this was also true.

"Besides," the Texans added through the voice of the *New York Herald,* "it is unthinkable to snub a state that grows the best cotton in the country, produces the best oak for ship construction, contains magnificent coal deposits, and has iron mines whose yield is fifty percent pure ore."

To this the *American Review* answered that, while the soil of Florida was not as rich, it would be better for molding and casting the cannon because it was composed of sand and clayey earth.

"But," said the Texans, "before casting anything in a place, you have to get there first, and travel to Florida is difficult, while the coast of Texas has Galveston Bay, which has thirty-five miles of coastline and is big enough to hold all the fleets in the world."

"You may as well forget about your Galveston Bay," replied the newspapers devoted to Florida, "because it's above the twenty-ninth parallel. But we have Tampa Bay, which opens south of the twenty-eighth parallel and enables ships to go directly to Tampa."

"A fine bay!" said Texas. "It's half silted up!"

"Silted up yourself!" retorted Florida. "Are you trying to insinuate that I'm a land of savages?"

"Well, it's true that the Seminoles still roam across you."

"What about your Apaches and Comanches? I suppose they're civilized!"

The war had been going on this way for several days when Florida tried to draw its adversary into another area. One morning the *Times* stated that since the project was "thoroughly American," it should take place only on "thoroughly American" land.

Texas was stung to the quick. "American!" it cried. "We're just as American as you are! Texas and Florida both became part of the Union in the same year: 1845!"

"Maybe so," said the *Times,* "but we'd belonged to the United States since 1820."

"You certainly had," said the *Tribune.* "After being Spanish or English for two hundred years, you were sold to the United States for five million dollars!"

"What of it?" said the Floridians. "It's nothing to be ashamed of. All the land in the Louisiana Purchase was bought from Napoleon in 1803 for only fifteen million dollars."

"It's disgraceful!" cried the Texans. "A wretched lump of land like Florida dares to compare itself to Texas, which instead of selling itself, won its independence by driving out the Mexicans on March 2, 1836, declared itself a republic after Sam Houston's victory over Santa Anna's troops on the banks of the San Jacinto, and later *voluntarily* joined the United States!"

"Because it was afraid of the Mexicans," said Florida.

Afraid! The word was much too strong. As soon as it was spoken the situation became intolerable. Everyone expected the two groups to fight a bloody battle in the streets of Baltimore at any moment. The authorities kept them under surveillance at all times.

Barbicane was at his wit's end. He was inundated with notes, documents, and threatening letters. What decision was he to make? From the standpoint of suitability of soil, ease of communication, and speed of transportation, the two states were truly equal. As for political considerations, they were irrelevant.

This hesitation and perplexity had lasted for a long time when Barbicane finally resolved to put an end to it. He summoned his colleagues to a meeting, and the solution he proposed to them was profoundly wise, as will be seen.

"In view of what's been happening between Florida

and Texas," he said, "it's obvious that the same difficulties will arise among the towns of whichever state is chosen. The rivalry will simply pass from the genus to the species, from states to towns. Texas has eleven towns that meet all the necessary conditions. If Texas is chosen, they'll all fight for the honor of having the project, and they'll only make more trouble for us. But Florida has only one town, so I think our choice is clear: Florida and Tampa!"

When this decision was made public it was a crushing blow to the delegates from Texas. They flew into an indescribable rage and personally challenged each member of the Gun Club to a duel. Only one course of action was open to the city authorities, and they took it. A special train was assembled; the Texans were put aboard it whether they liked it or not, and they then left the city at a speed of thirty miles an hour.

Despite the rapidity of their departure, they still had time to hurl one last sarcastic and threatening remark at their adversaries. Referring to the narrowness of the Florida peninsula, they claimed it would not be able to withstand the shock of such a great explosion and would be blown to pieces the first time the cannon was fired.

"Then let it be blown to pieces!" the Floridians replied with a laconicism worthy of ancient times.

CHAPTER 12

URBI ET ORBI

ONCE THE astronomical, mechanical, and geographical difficulties had been resolved, the question of money arose. An enormous sum would have to be procured for the project. The necessary millions could not be provided by any single person, or even by any single country.

Therefore, although the project was American, Barbicane decided to make it a worldwide undertaking by asking for the financial cooperation of every nation. It was both the right and the duty of the whole world to take a hand in the affairs of its satellite. The subscription that was opened for that purpose extended from Baltimore to the whole world, *urbi et orbi.*

This subscription was to succeed beyond all expectations, even though the money was donated, not lent. It was purely a disinterested operation which offered no chance of profit.

But the effect of Barbicane's announcement had not stopped at the borders of the United States: it had crossed the Atlantic and the Pacific, invading Asia, Europe, Africa, and Oceania. American observatories immediately entered into communication with foreign observatories. Some of the latter—those in Paris, St. Petersburg, Capetown, Berlin, Altona, Stockholm, Warsaw, Hamburg,

Buda, Bologna, Malta, Lisbon, Benares, Madras, and Peking—sent their congratulations to the Gun Club. The others waited cautiously.

As for the Greenwich Observatory, it took a firm stand that was supported by the twenty-two other astronomical establishments in Great Britain: it boldly denied the possibility of success, and stated its agreement with Captain Nicholl's theories. Thus, while various learned societies were promising to send representatives to Tampa, the Greenwich staff held a meeting at which Barbicane's proposal was unceremoniously brushed aside. It was simply a matter of English jealousy, and nothing else.

All in all, the reaction was excellent in the scientific world, and from there it passed to the masses, who, in general, were keenly interested in the project. This was an important fact, since the masses were going to be called upon to subscribe a large capital.

On October 8, Barbicane had issued an enthusiastic manifesto in which he appealed to "all men of good will on earth." This document, translated into all languages, was highly successful.

Subscriptions were opened in the main cities of the United States, with a central office in the Bank of Baltimore, at 9 Baltimore Street, and were then opened in various countries on both sides of the Atlantic, with the following firms:

VIENNA: *S. M. Rothschild*
SAINT PETERSBURG: *Stieglitz & Co.*
PARIS: *Crédit Mobilier*
STOCKHOLM: *Tottie & Arfuredson*
LONDON: *N. M. Rothschild & Son*
TURIN: *Ardouin & Co.*
GENEVA: *Lompard, Odier & Co.*

CONSTANTINOPLE: *the Ottoman Bank*
BRUSSELS: *S. Lambert*
MADRID: *Daniel Weisweller*
AMSTERDAM: *the Netherlands Credit Association*
ROME: *Torlonia & Co.*
LISBON: *Lecesne & Co.*
COPENHAGEN: *the Private Bank*
BUENOS AIRES: *the Maua Bank*
RIO DE JANEIRO: *same firm*
MONTEVIDEO: *same firm*
VALPARAISO: *Thomas La Chambre & Co.*
MEXICO CITY: *Matrin Darin & Co.*
LIMA: *Thomas La Chambre & Co.*

Within three days after Barbicane's manifesto, four million dollars had been deposited in the different American cities. With such a first installment, the Gun Club was already able to get under way.

A few days later there were dispatches telling America that the foreign subscriptions had been eagerly covered. Some countries had distinguished themselves by their generosity; others did not loosen their purse strings so easily. It was a matter of temperament.

Figures are more eloquent than words, so here is the official tabulation of the sums that were deposited to the account of the Gun Club after the subscription was closed:

For her share, Russia paid the enormous sum of 368,733 rubles ($272,875). This will be surprising only if one is unfamiliar with the Russians' strong scientific inclination and the progress they have made in astronomical studies, thanks to their many observatories, the most important one of which cost two million rubles.

France began by laughing at the Americans' pretensions.

The moon served as a pretext for countless tired puns and a score of vaudeville numbers whose bad taste was equaled only by the ignorance they displayed. But just as the French formerly paid after having sung, they now paid after having laughed, and they subscribed the sum of 1,253,932 francs ($231,980). At that price they were entitled to a little merriment.

Austria showed sufficient generosity in the midst of her financial troubles. Her contribution was 216,000 florins ($96,200), which was welcome.

Sweden and Norway contributed 52,000 rixdalers ($54,450). It was a large sum in relation to the population, but would surely have been still larger if the subscription had taken place in Christiania as well as in Stockholm. For one reason or another, the Norwegians do not like to send their money to Sweden.

Prussia showed her approval of the project by sending 250,000 thalers ($173,440). Her observatories readily contributed a sizable sum and were the most ardent in encouraging Barbicane.

Turkey behaved generously, but she had a personal interest in the matter: the moon governs the course of her years and her fast of Ramadan. She could do no less than to give 1,372,640 piasters ($63,300), although she gave it with an eagerness which betrayed a certain pressure from the Ottoman government.

Belgium distinguished herself among the smaller countries by a gift of 513,000 francs ($94,900), or a little more than two cents per inhabitant.

Holland and her colonies put 10,000 florins ($43,500) into the project, asking only that they be given a five-percent discount, since they were paying cash.

Although a little cramped in her territory, Denmark

gave 9,000 ducats ($21,720), which proves the Danes' love of scientific expeditions.

The Germanic Confederation agreed to give 34,385 florins ($13,320). She could not have been asked for more; and anyway, she would not have given it.

Italy, though in straitened circumstances, managed to scrape up 200,000 lire ($37,000) by turning her children's pockets inside out. If she had had Venetia she would have done better; but she did not have it.

The Papal States felt it their duty to contribute no less than 7,040 scudi ($7,030), and Portugal showed her devotion to science by a donation of 30,000 crusados ($20,940).

As for Mexico, her gift amounted to only $320, and she could scarcely afford even that small sum; an empire that has just been founded is always a little short of cash.

Switzerland's modest contribution to the American project was 257 francs ($47). It must be said frankly that she did not see the practical side of the operation. It seemed unlikely to her that shooting a shell to the moon would result in the establishment of business relations with it, and she felt it would be imprudent to place any considerable amount of her capital in such a hazardous undertaking. And, after all, she may have been right.

As for Spain, it was impossible for her to get together more than 110 reals ($11). She gave as her excuse that she had her railroads to finish. The truth is that science is not very highly regarded in Spain. She is still a little backward. Furthermore, there were some Spaniards, and they were not among the least educated, who did not have a clear idea of the relation between the mass of the projectile and that of the moon; they were afraid the projectile might alter the moon's orbit, make it cease to be a satellite and bring it crashing into the earth. Under such circumstances they felt it would be better to do nothing, and, practically speaking, that was what they did.

There was still England. We have already noted the contemptuous hostility with which she greeted Barbicane's proposal. The twenty-five million people who live in Great Britain have a single soul. They maintained that the Gun Club's project was contrary to the principle of nonintervention, and they refused to give one farthing to it. On hearing this news, the members of the Gun Club shrugged their shoulders and went on with their great enterprise.

When South America—that is, Peru, Chile, Brazil, Colombia, and the provinces of La Plata—had given $300,000 as her share, the Gun Club had a considerable amount of capital at its disposal: $4,000,000 from the American subscriptions and $1,410,143 from the foreign ones for a total of $5,410,143.

The size of this sum should not be surprising. According to the estimates, the money would be almost completely absorbed by the work of casting and boring, masonry, transporting the workers and providing them with living quarters in an almost uninhabited region, constructing furnaces and buildings, equipping factories, the powder, the projectile, and incidental expenses. During the Civil War there were cannon shots that cost a thousand dollars apiece; Barbicane's shot, unique in the annals of artillery, could easily cost five thousand times as much.

On October 20 a contract was signed with the Cold Spring factory, near New York City, which had supplied Parrott with his best cast-iron cannons during the war.

It was stipulated in the contract that the management of the company would assume the responsibility of transporting the iron for the casting to Tampa. This operation was to be terminated by October 15 of the following year, and the cannon was to be completed and in good condition, under penalty of an indemnity of a hundred dollars a day, until the next time when the moon would be in the same conditions, that is, in eighteen years and eleven days. The company would also be responsible for hiring and paying the workers, and making all necessary arrangements.

Two copies of this contract were signed by I. Barbicane, president of the Gun Club, and J. Murchison, manager of the Cold Spring Company, after both men had given their approval to its terms.

CHAPTER 13

STONE HILL

AFTER THE Gun Club had decided against Texas, there was no one in the United States, where everyone knows how to read, who did not feel duty-bound to study the geography of Florida. The bookstores had never sold so many copies of Bartram's *Travel in Florida,* Roman's *Natural History of East and West Florida,* Williams' *The Territory of Florida,* and Cleland's *On the Culture of Sugar Cane in East Florida.* New editions had to be printed. They were bought up with frenzied haste.

Barbicane had better things to do than read: he wanted to make the site of the cannon and see it with his own eyes. Without wasting a single moment, he turned over to the Cambridge Observatory the funds necessary for the construction of a telescope and negotiated a contract with Breadwill & Co. of Albany for the manufacture of an aluminum projectile. Then he left Baltimore, accompanied by J. T. Maston, Major Elphiston, and Mr. Murchison, manager of the Cold Spring Company.

They reached New Orleans the next day. There they immediately boarded the *Tampico,* a navy dispatch boat which the government had placed at their disposal. They left the harbor with a full head of steam and the coast of Louisiana soon vanished behind them.

The voyage was not long. Two days after their departure, having covered 480 miles, they sighted the coast of Florida. As they approached it, Barbicane saw that the land was low, flat, and rather barren-looking. After passing several coves rich in oysters and lobsters, the *Tampico* entered Tampa Bay.

The upper end of this bay is divided into two sections. The *Tampico* soon steamed into the eastern one. A short time later, the low batteries of Fort Brooke came into view, then the town of Tampa appeared, casually spread out at the far end of the little natural harbor formed by the mouth of the Hillsborough River.

It was there that the *Tampico* dropped anchor on October 22, at seven o'clock in the evening. The four passengers immediately went ashore.

Barbicane felt his heart pounding when he set foot on Florida soil. He seemed to be testing it, like an architect testing the solidity of a house. J. T. Maston scratched the ground with his hook.

"Gentlemen," said Barbicane, "we have no time to lose. Tomorrow we'll explore the region on horseback."

As soon as he had stepped ashore, the three thousand inhabitants of Tampa had come forward to meet him. It was an honor he was fully entitled to for having favored them with his choice. They received him with a formidable outburst of cheering, but he hurried away to a room in the Hotel Franklin and refused to see anyone. The role of a famous man did not suit him at all.

The next morning, October 23, a group of little Spanish horses, full of vigor and fire, were prancing beneath his windows. But instead of four, there were fifty, and they had riders. Barbicane and his three companions went downstairs. At first he was surprised to find himself in the midst of such a cavalcade. He noticed that each rider had a rifle slung over his shoulder and a brace of pistols in his saddle holsters. The reason for this array of armed strength was soon given by a young Floridian who said to him:

"It's because of the Seminoles, sir."

"What are you talking about?"

"They're wild Indians. We thought it would be better if we escorted you."

"Ridiculous!" said J. T. Maston as he mounted his horse.

"Well, it's safer," said the Floridian.

"Thank you for your thoughtfulness, gentlemen," said Barbicane. "And now, let's go."

The little troop set off immediately and vanished in a cloud of dust. It was five o'clock in the morning. The sun was already shining and the temperature was eighty-four, but the heat was softened by a cool sea breeze.

After leaving Tampa, Barbicane rode southward, following the coast until he came to Alifia Creek. This little stream empties into the bay twelve miles below Tampa. Barbicane and his escort rode eastward along its right bank. The bay soon disappeared behind a rise in the ground and the Florida landscape filled their whole field of vision.

Florida is divided into two parts. The northern one is more populous and less wild. Its capital is Tallahassee, and one of the main American naval dockyards is at Pensacola. The other part, pressed between the Atlantic and the Gulf of Mexico, is only a slender peninsula washed by the Gulf Stream, a tip of land, lost in the midst of a little archipelago, which is constantly being passed by the many ships on their way to and from the Old Bahama Channel. It is the advanced sentinel against the violent hurricanes that attack the Gulf. The state's area is

38,033,267 acres, among which Barbicane had to find one that was located below the twenty-eighth parallel and suitable for his project; and so, as he rode along, he attentively examined the configuration and composition of the ground.

Florida, discovered by Juan Ponce de Leon in 1512, on Palm Sunday, was first named "Flowery Easter" in Spanish. It did not deserve this charming name on its hot, arid coasts. But a few miles inland the nature of the terrain gradually changed, and the region showed itself to be worthy of its name. It was interlaced with creeks and rivers, and studded with ponds and little lakes. The landscape was not unlike that of Holland or Guiana. Then the land began to rise and soon showed its cultivated plains in which all sorts of northern and southern crops were flourishing, its immense fields where the tropical sun and the water conserved in the clay of the soil did most of the work of cultivation, and finally its fields of pineapples, sweet potatoes, tobacco, rice, cotton, and sugar cane, stretching out as far as the eye could see, displaying their wealth with carefree prodigality.

Barbicane seemed glad to note the gradual rising of the ground. When J. T. Maston asked him about it he said, "It's very important for us to cast our cannon on high ground."

"So it will be closer to the moon?"

"No," said Barbicane, smiling. "What difference would a few feet make? But on high ground our work will be easier: we won't have to fight against water, and so we won't need a long, expensive casing. That's something to consider when you're digging a hole nine hundred feet deep."

"You're right," said Murchison. "We must avoid water as much as possible during the digging. But if we come to

underground springs it won't bother us: we'll either
change their course or pump them dry with our machines.
We won't be digging a dark, narrow artesian well,* where
the drill, the casing, the sounding-rod, and all the other
well-digger's tools have to work blindly. No, we'll be
working in the open air, in broad daylight, with picks and
mattocks, and with the help of blasting we'll get our work
done quickly."

"Even so," said Barbicane, "if the elevation or the nature of the soil spares us the trouble of dealing with underground water, the work will be done faster and better."

"That's true, Mr. Barbicane, and unless I'm mistaken
we'll find a good spot before long."

"I wish we were ready to begin digging now!"

"And I wish we were ready to finish!" cried J. T.
Maston.

"We'll get there, gentlemen," said Murchison, "and believe me, the Cold Spring Company won't have to pay a
cent for being late."

"I hope not, for your sake!" said J. T. Maston. "Do you
realize that a hundred dollars a day for eighteen years and
eleven days, which is how long it will be before the moon
is in the same conditions again, comes to $658,100?"

"No, I didn't know that, and we won't need to know it."

By ten o'clock in the morning the little troop had rid-
den a dozen miles. The fertile fields were succeeded by a
forest in which a wide variety of trees grew in tropical
profusion. This almost impenetrable forest was composed of masses of vines and pomegranate, orange,
lemon, fig, olive, apricot, and banana trees, whose fruit
and blossoms rivaled one another in color and aroma. In
the fragrant shade of those magnificent trees a whole

*It took nine years to dig the Grenelle well; it is 1,794 feet deep.

world of brightly colored birds were singing and flying. Among them were boatbills, whose nest should be a jewel case in order to be worthy of them.

J. T. Maston and Major Elphiston could not see that opulent forest without admiring its magnificent beauties. But Barbicane was insensitive to those wonders. He was impatient to move on. That fertile region displeased him because of its very fertility; although he was not a dowser, he sensed water beneath his feet, and he vainly looked for signs of incontestable dryness.

They rode on. They had to ford several streams, and this was not without danger, for the water was infested with alligators fifteen to eighteen feet long. J. T. Maston boldly threatened them with his formidable hook, but he succeeded in frightening only the pelicans, ducks, tropic birds, and other wild inhabitants of the banks, while the big red flamingos stared blankly at him.

Finally these wet-country denizens disappeared. The trees became smaller and less dense, until finally there were only isolated clumps of them on a vast plain where startled deer raced away from the riders.

"At last!" said Barbicane, standing up in his stirrups. "Here's a region of pine trees!"

"And Indians, too," said the major.

A few Seminoles had appeared on the horizon. They moved excitedly, rode back and forth on their swift horses, brandished long spears and fired rifles whose reports were muffled by distance, but they limited themselves to these hostile demonstrations. Barbicane and his companions were not alarmed.

They were now in the middle of a broad, rocky, sundrenched open space several acres in area. It was higher than the surrounding land and seemed to offer all the conditions required for the site of the Gun Club's cannon.

"Stop!" said Barbicane, reining his horse. "Does this place have a name?"

"It's called Stone Hill," replied one of the Floridians. Barbicane dismounted without a word, took out his instruments and began determining his position with extreme precision. His companions, gathered around him, watched him in deep silence.

The sun was just then passing the meridian. A short time later, Barbicane quickly calculated the results of his observations and said:

"This place is 1800 feet above sea level, latitude 27° 7' north, longitude 5° 7' west.* Its dryness and rockiness seem to indicate all the conditions favorable to our project, so it's here that we'll build our powder magazines, our workshops, our furnaces, and the houses for our workers, and it will be from here, from this very spot," he said emphatically, stamping his foot on Stone Hill, "that our projectile will begin its journey through space to the moon!"

*From the meridian of Washington.

CHAPTER 14

PICK AND TROWEL

THAT EVENING Barbicane and his companions returned to Tampa. Murchison went back on board the *Tampico* to go to New Orleans. He was to hire an army of workers and bring back the major part of the material. Barbicane and Maston would remain in Tampa in order to organize the preliminary work with the aid of the local people.

Eight days after her departure, the *Tampico* came back into the bay with a fleet of steamships. Murchison had collected fifteen hundred workers. In the evil days of slavery he would have wasted his time and effort, but now that America, the land of freedom, had only free men within her borders, they were willing to go any place where there were well-paid jobs. The Gun Club was not short of money; it offered its men high wages and generous bonuses. Any man who signed up to work in Florida could count on a considerable sum of money being deposited in his name in the Bank of Baltimore when the project was completed. Murchison therefore had a wide choice and was able to set high standards of intelligence and skill for his workers. There is every reason to believe that he filled his working legion with the finest mechanics, firemen, smelters, smiths, miners, brickmakers, and laborers of all kinds, black and white, without distinction of color. Many of them brought their families with them. It was a veritable emigration.

On October 31, at ten o'clock in the morning, this troop landed at Tampa. It is easy to imagine the agitation and activity which reigned in that small town, whose population had been doubled in one day. Tampa was to gain enormously from the Gun Club's project, not because of the workers, who were immediately taken to Stone Hill, but because of the influx of curious people who gradually converged on the Florida peninsula from all parts of the world.

During the first few days attention was centered on unloading the cargoes of the fleet; tools, machines, food supplies, and a large number of sheet-iron houses dismantled into numbered pieces. At the same time, Barbicane laid out the route of a fifteen-mile railroad between Tampa and Stone Hill.

The way in which an American railroad is constructed is well known: whimsical in its meanderings, bold in its slopes, climbing hills and plunging into valleys, it runs blindly, with no concern for a straight line. It is neither costly nor troublesome, but its trains jump the track with gay abandon. The line between Tampa and Stone Hill was only a trifle and required little time and money for its construction.

Barbicane was the soul of that little community of people who had answered his call. He communicated his driving energy, enthusiasm, and conviction to them. He seemed to be everywhere at once, as though he were endowed with the gift of ubiquity, and he was always followed by J. T. Maston, his buzzing fly. His practical mind turned out countless ingenious inventions. With him there were no obstacles, no difficulties, no perplexities; he had an answer to every question, a solution to every problem.

He carried on an active correspondence with the Gun Club and the Cold Spring Company. Day and night, with a full head of steam, the *Tampico* awaited his orders in the harbor.

On November 1 he left Tampa with a group of workers. The next day, a town of sheet-iron houses rose around Stone Hill. A stockade was built around it, and from its bustle and animation it might have been one of the biggest cities in the country. Life in it was regulated with discipline, and the work was begun in perfect order.

After careful drillings had revealed the nature of the soil, digging was begun on November 4. On that day, Barbicane called his foremen together and said to them:

"My friends, you all know why I've brought you to this wild part of Florida. We're going to cast a cannon with an inside diameter of nine feet and walls six feet thick, surrounded by a layer of stone nineteen and a half feet thick, so the hole we're going to dig will be sixty feet wide and nine hundred feet deep. It's a big job, and it must be finished in a little more than eight months. You'll have to take out 2,542,400 cubic feet of earth in 255 days, or about 10,000 cubic feet a day. That wouldn't be hard for a thousand men working with plenty of elbowroom; it won't be so easy in a rather tight space. But it must be done, and it *will* be done. I'm counting on your courage as much as on your skill."

At eight o'clock in the morning the first pick struck the soil of Florida, and from then on that valiant tool was never idle in the hands of the diggers. They worked around the clock in six-hour shifts.

However colossal the operation may have been, it did not surpass the limits of human strength; far from it. How many undertakings whose difficulties were more real, and in which the elements had to be combatted directly, have been brought to completion! To speak only of similar projects, it will be enough to cite "Father Joseph's Well," dug near Cairo by Sultan Saladin at a time when machines had not yet increased man's strength a hundredfold: it descends three hundred feet below the level of the Nile. And then there is the six-hundred-foot well dug at Coblentz by Margrave Johann of Baden. All that Barbicane's men had to do was to triple the depth of Saladin's well and make it ten times wider, which would make digging easy. There was not one foreman or laborer who had any doubt about the success of the operation.

The work was speeded up by an important decision made by Murchison, with Barbicane's approval. A clause in the contract specified that the cannon was to be reinforced by bands of wrought iron put in place while they were still hot. This was a useless precaution, because it was obvious that the cannon could do without those rings. The clause was canceled.

This made it possible to save a great deal of time, for they were now able to use the new system of digging that has been adopted for wells, in which the masonry is made at the same time as the hole. Thanks to this simple procedure, it is no longer necessary to shore up the earth with braces: the masonry contains it with unshakable strength, and moves itself down by its own weight.

This operation was not to begin until the digging had reached the solid part of the ground.

On November 4, fifty workers dug a circular hole with a diameter of sixty feet at the center of the stockaded enclosure, that is, at the top of Stone Hill.

First they encountered a six-inch layer of black vegetable mold which they went through easily. Then came two feet of fine sand which was carefully taken out, for it was to be used in making the inner mold.

After this sand came four feet of rather compact white clay which resembled the marl in England.

Then the picks struck sparks from a kind of hard, dry, very solid rock, composed of petrified seashells, which they were to struggle against until the end of the digging. At this point the hole was six and a half feet deep, and the masonry work was begun.

At the bottom of this excavation they built an oak disk, firmly bolted and enormously strong, with a hole in its center that had the same diameter as the outer diameter of the cannon. It was on this disk that they built the first courses of masonry, whose stones were held together with inflexible tenacity by hydraulic cement. When they had made stonework from the outer edge to the inner circle, the workers were enclosed in a round pit twenty-one feet across.

Next they took up their picks and mattocks again and began digging under the disk, carefully supporting it with extremely strong blocks. Each time the hole had become two feet deeper, they successively took out the blocks; the disk would then gradually sink, taking with it the massive ring of stonework on top of which the masons were constantly working, not forgetting to make vent holes through which the gas could escape during the casting operation.

This kind of work required great skill and unremitting attention. More than one worker was seriously or even fatally injured by falling stones while digging under the disk. But their zeal never flagged for one minute, day or night. During the day, by the light of a sun that raised the temperature of that scorched plain to ninety-nine degrees a few months later, and at night, beneath the white glow of the electric lights, the noise of the picks striking rock, the explosion of blasting charges, the clanking of machinery, and swirls of smoke in the air traced around Stone Hill a circle of terror that herds of buffalo and groups of Seminoles did not dare to cross.

Meanwhile the work advanced regularly. Steam cranes speeded the removal of earth. There was little concern for unexpected obstacles. Only foreseen difficulties were encountered, and they were skillfully overcome.

By the end of the first month the pit had reached its scheduled depth of 112 feet. In December this depth was doubled, and in January it was tripled. In February the workers had to combat underground springs that welled up from beneath the surface. Powerful pumps and compressed-air equipment had to be used to draw them off in order to stop up their openings with concrete, as one stops up a leak in a ship. Finally those undesirable streams were mastered. But because of the looseness of the earth, the disk sank on one side and part of the stonework collapsed. Imagine the awesome weight of that stone ring 450 feet high! This accident cost the lives of several workers.

It took three weeks to shore up the stonework, build a support beneath it, and restore the disk to its original position. But thanks to the skill of the engineers and the power of the machines employed, the endangered construction recovered its balance and the excavation continued.

The work was not interrupted by any other incidents. On June 10, twenty days before the date set by Barbicane, the pit, completely sheathed in masonry, reached its final depth of nine hundred feet. At the bottom the stonework rested on a massive thirty-foot cube, while its top was level with the surface of the ground.

Barbicane and the other members of the Gun Club

warmly congratulated Murchison. His herculean task had been carried out with extraordinary rapidity.

During those eight months, Barbicane had not left Stone Hill for one moment. As he had kept close watch on the digging operations, he had been constantly concerned with the health and welfare of his workers, and he was fortunate enough to avoid those epidemics that are common to aggregations of men, and are so disastrous in regions exposed to tropical influences.

Several workers, it is true, paid with their lives for the rashness that is inherent in such dangerous work; but those deplorable accidents are impossible to avoid, and Americans are not inclined to worry about such details. They care more about mankind in general than about the individual in particular. Barbicane professed contrary principles, however, and applied them at every opportunity. Because of his care, his intelligence, his useful intervention in dangerous cases, and his deep, humane wisdom, the accident rate did not go beyond that of European countries noted for their abundant precautions, including France, where there is an average of one accident for every 200,000 francs' worth of work.

CHAPTER 15

THE FESTIVAL OF CASTING

DURING THE eight months that were spent on the excavation, the preparatory work for the casting had been done simultaneously and with great speed. A stranger arriving at Stone Hill would have been amazed by what he saw.

Arranged in a circle around the pit with a radius of 600 yards were 1,200 reverberatory furnaces six feet wide and three feet apart. The circumference of this circle of furnaces was over two miles. They were all built to the same design, with a high rectangular chimney, and they produced a singular effect. J. T. Maston felt that it was a magnificent architectural arrangement. It reminded him of the monuments of Washington. For him, there was nothing more beautiful anywhere in the world, not even in Greece, where, he freely admitted, he had never been.

It will be remembered that in its third meeting the committee had decided to use cast iron, specifically the kind known as "gray," to make the cannon. This metal is tougher, more ductile, easier to bore, and suitable for all casting operations. Melted with coal, it is of superior quality for things that require great strength, such as cannons, steam engine cylinders, hydraulic presses, etc.

But it is seldom homogenous enough when it has been

melted only once. It takes a second melting to purify and refine it by ridding it of all its earthy residues.

Therefore, before being sent to Tampa, the iron ore, melted in the blast furnaces at Cold Spring and placed in contact with heated carbon and silicon, was carburized and transformed into cast iron.* After this operation, the metal was sent to Stone Hill. But 136,000,000 pounds of iron would have been too expensive to send by rail: the transportation charges would have doubled the cost of the iron. It seemed preferable to charter ships in New York and load them with the iron in bars. It took no less than sixty-eight ships with a capacity of a thousand tons each, a veritable fleet. On May 3 they left New York harbor, headed out to sea, moved southward along the coast to the Straits of Florida, rounded the tip of the peninsula and steamed into Tampa Bay on May 10. They all moored in the port of Tampa without incident.

There the metal was unloaded from the ships and placed in the cars of the Stone Hill railroad. By the middle of January all of the enormous mass had reached its destination.

It will easily be seen that the 1,200 furnaces were not more than was needed to melt that 70,000-ton mass of metal all at once. Each furnace could contain about 114,000 pounds of metal. They had been made on the same pattern as those that had been used in casting the Rodman cannon: they had a trapezoidal shape and were very low. The heating apparatus and the chimney were at opposite ends of the furnace, so that it was equally heated over its entire length. These furnaces, made of firebrick, were composed only of a grate for burning the coal and a

---

*It is by removing this carbon and silicon in the refining operation in a puddling furnace that cast iron is transformed into ductile iron.

hearth on which the bars of iron were laid. This hearth, inclined at an angle of twenty-five degrees, enabled the molten metal to flow into basins, from which 1,200 converging gutters would take it to the central pit.

The day after the pit had been completed, Barbicane gave orders to begin work on the inner mold. A cylinder nine hundred feet high, with a diameter of nine feet, had to be placed inside the pit, so that it would exactly fill the space reserved for the bore of the cannon. This cylinder was composed of a mixture of clayey earth and sand to which hay and straw had been added. The space left between the mold and the stonework was to be filled by the molten metal, which would thus form walls six feet thick.

To hold the cylinder upright, it had to be stiffened with iron reinforcements and steadied by crosspieces sealed into the stonework. After the casting these crosspieces would remain inside the metal and would have no harmful effect on it.

This operation was completed on July 8 and the casting was scheduled for the next day.

"Our festival of casting is going to be a beautiful ceremony!" J. T. Maston said to his friend Barbicane.

"No doubt," replied Barbicane, "but it won't be a public ceremony."

"What! You're not going to open the enclosure to anyone who wants to come in?"

"Of course not. Casting the cannon will be a delicate operation, to say nothing of its danger, and I prefer to have it done behind closed doors. When the projectile is fired you can have a festival if you want, but not till then."

Barbicane was right: the operation might present unexpected dangers, and a large crowd of onlookers might make it impossible to take effective countermeasures. Those involved in the operation would have to keep their freedom of movement. No one, therefore, was allowed inside the enclosure, except for a group of Gun Club members who had made the trip to Tampa. The group included the dashing Bilsby, Tom Hunter, Colonel Bloomsberry, Major Elphiston, General Morgan, and others. For them, the casting of the cannon was a personal matter. J. T. Maston was appointed to be their guide. He spared them no detail; he took them everywhere—to the powder magazines, the workshops, the machines—and he made them inspect the 1,200 furnaces one after another. By the time they had made their 1,200th inspection their interest had dulled a little.

The casting was to take place at noon. The day before, each furnace had been loaded with 114,000 pounds of metal in bars, arranged in crosshatch stacks so that the hot air could circulate freely among them. The 1,200 chimneys had been spewing their torrents of flame into the air since morning, while the ground was being shaken by dull tremors. For each pound of metal to be melted, a pound of coal had to be burned, so 70,000 tons of coal sent up a thick curtain of black smoke before the sun.

The heat soon became unbearable inside the circle of furnaces, whose roaring was like the rumble of thunder. Powerful blowers added their noise as they saturated the glowing furnaces with oxygen.

To succeed, this operation would have to be carried out rapidly. At the signal given by the firing of a cannon, each furnace was to release its molten metal and empty itself entirely.

When all the preparations had been made, the workers and supervisors waited for the signal with impatient excitement. There was no one in the enclosure now, and each casting foreman was at his post beside the tapholes.

Barbicane and his colleagues watched the operation

from a nearby knoll. Before them was a cannon ready to be fired at a sign from Murchison.

A few minutes before noon, the first drops of metal began to flow. The basins gradually filled, and when the metal was entirely liquid it was kept at rest for a time, in order to facilitate the separation of foreign substances.

At exactly noon the cannon fired, throwing its tawny lightning into the air. Twelve hundred tapholes opened at once, and 1,200 snakes of fire crawled toward the central pit, straightening their incandescent coils. There, with a fearful uproar, they plunged to a depth of nine hundred feet. It was a moving and magnificent spectacle. The ground quivered while those cascades of metal, sending whirlwinds of smoke toward the sky, volatilized the moisture in the mold and shot it through the vent holes in the stonework in the form of dense vapor. These artificial clouds spiraled up to an altitude of 3,000 feet. An Indian wondering beyond the horizon might have believed that a new volcano was being formed in Florida, but this was not an eruption, a tornado, a storm, a struggle of the elements, or any of the other terrible phenomena that nature is capable of producing. No, it was man alone who had created those reddish vapors, those gigantic flames worthy of a volcano, those loud tremors that brought an earthquake to mind, that roar which could rival any hurricane, and it was his hand that had precipitated, into an abyss that he himself had dug, a whole Niagara of molten metal.

CHAPTER 16

THE CANNON

HAD THE casting operation been successful? No one could do anything more than make conjectures. There was every reason to believe it had been successful, however, since the mold had absorbed the entire mass of metal that had been melted in the furnaces. In any case, it would be impossible to make any direct verification for a long time.

When Major Rodman cast his 160,000-pound cannon, the cooling process took no less than fifteen days. How long, then, was the Gun Club's monstrous cannon, wreathed in swirls of vapor and defended by its intense heat, going to be hidden from its admirers' gaze? It was difficult to calculate.

Meanwhile the patience of the Gun Club members was being put to a strenuous test. But there was nothing to be done about it. J. T. Maston's devotion nearly caused him to be roasted alive. Two weeks after the casting, an immense plume of smoke was still rising into the sky and the ground was too hot to stand on within a radius of two hundred yards around the top of Stone Hill.

Days went by, weeks followed one another. There was no way to cool the immense cylinder. It was impossible to go near it. There was nothing to do but wait, and the members of the Gun Club fretted anxiously.

"It's already August 10!" J. T. Maston said one morning. "Less than four months till December! And we still have to take out the core, ream the bore of the cannon, and load it! We won't be ready! We can't even go near the cannon! Isn't it ever going to cool? What a cruel joke it would be if it didn't cool in time!"

The impatient secretary's friends tried to calm him, without success. Barbicane said nothing, but his silence concealed an inner irritation. Being stopped by an obstacle that could be surmounted only by time, a formidable enemy under the circumstances, and being at the mercy of an adversary was hard for a seasoned warrior to endure.

Daily observations finally revealed a change in the state of the ground. By August 15 the rising vapors had diminished noticeably in intensity and thickness. A few days later, the ground was exhaling only a light mist, the last breath of the monster enclosed in its stone coffin. The tremors of the ground slowly died down and the circle of heat shrank. The more impatient onlookers moved closer. One day they gained ten feet, then twenty feet the next day. On August 22, Barbicane, the other members of the Gun Club, and Murchison were able to stand on the ring of iron at the top of Stone Hill. It was surely a healthy place, for it was impossible to have cold feet there.

"At last!" Barbicane exclaimed with a great sigh of satisfaction.

Work was resumed that same day. The first step was to take out the inner mold in order to free the bore of the cannon. Picks, mattocks, and drilling equipment were in motion day and night. The clayey earth and sand had been made extremely hard by the heat, but with the aid of machines, the workers overcame that mixture, which was still hot from contact with the cast-iron walls of the cannon. The matter removed was rapidly taken away in railroad cars. The men worked so hard, Barbicane urged them on so earnestly, and his arguments were presented with such great force, in the form of dollars, that by September 3 all traces of the mold had vanished.

The reaming operation was immediately begun. The machines were installed without delay, and swiftly moved powerful reamers whose cutting edges bit into the rough surface of the cast iron. A few weeks later the inner surface of the immense tube was perfectly cylindrical and smooth.

Finally, on September 22, less than a year after Barbicane's announcement, the enormous cannon's verticality and inner dimensions were checked by delicate instruments and it was pronounced ready for action. There was nothing to do now but wait for the moon, and everyone was sure it would arrive on time.

J. T. Maston's joy was boundless. He nearly had a disastrous fall when he looked down into the nine-hundred-foot tube. If it had not been for Bloomsberry's right arm, which the worthy colonel had fortunately kept, Maston, like a new Erostratus, would have met death in the depths of the cannon.

The cannon was finished. There could no longer be any doubt that it would turn out perfectly, so on October 6 Captain Nicholl reluctantly paid his bet and Barbicane entered the sum of two thousand dollars in his books. We may assume that the captain was angry to the point of being ill. However, he still had bets of three, four, and five thousand dollars, and if he could win two of them he would still come out fairly well. But money was not his concern; his rival's success in casting a cannon that not even fifty-foot armor could have withstood was a terrible blow to him.

Since September 23 the enclosure at Stone Hill had been open to the public. It is not difficult to imagine the influx of visitors that took place.

Swarms of people from all over the country converged on Florida. The town of Tampa had grown prodigiously during the year it had devoted entirely to the work of the Gun Club, and it now had a population of 150,000. After having swallowed up Fort Brooke in a maze of streets, it was now stretching out onto the tongue of land that divides the bay into two parts. New neighborhoods, new squares, and a whole forest of houses had sprung up on those formerly deserted shores, in the warmth of the American sun. Companies had been formed for the construction of churches, schools, and private dwellings, and in less than a year the area of the town increased tenfold.

It is well known that the Yankees are born businessmen. Wherever fate leads them, from the tropics to the far north, their business instinct must find some useful outlet. That is why people who had come to Florida entirely out of curiosity, to watch the operations of the Gun Club, let themselves be drawn into business ventures as soon as they settled down in Tampa. The ships that had been chartered for transporting workers and material had made the port an incredibly busy one. Soon other ships, of all shapes and sizes, laden with food, supplies, and merchandise, were moving across the bay. Shipowners and brokers established large offices in the town, and every day the *Shipping Gazette* reported new arrivals in the port of Tampa.

Roads multiplied around the town and, in view of the amazing growth of its population and business, it was finally connected by rail with the southern states of the Union. A railroad joined Mobile and Pensacola, the great southern naval dockyard; then, from this important point, it went on to Tallahassee. There it met a small section of track, twenty-one miles long, by which Tallahassee was connected with Saint Marks, on the coast. This section was extended to Tampa, and on its way it revived and awakened the dead or sleeping parts of central Florida. Thus Tampa, thanks to those wonders of industry which sprang from an idea that had hatched in a man's brain one day, was rightfully able to take on the airs of a big city. It had been nicknamed "Moon City," and the capital of Florida went into a total eclipse, visible from all over the world.

It will now be easy to understand why the rivalry between Texas and Florida was so great, and why the Texans were so irritated when their claims were dismissed by the Gun Club's choice. In their farsighted wisdom they had realized what a region could gain from Barbicane's project, and the benefits that would flow from such a mighty cannon shot. Texas had lost a great business center, railroads, and a considerable growth in population. All these advantages had gone to that wretched Florida peninsula, lying like a breakwater between the Atlantic and the Gulf of Mexico. Barbicane was therefore no more popular in Texas than General Santa Anna.

Meanwhile, despite its commercial and industrial ardor, Tampa was far from forgetting the Gun Club's fascinating operations. On the contrary, its inhabitants took deep interest in the smallest details of the project and in every stroke of a pick. There was constant travel back and forth between the town and Stone Hill; it was a veritable procession, or, better still, a pilgrimage.

It could already be foreseen that on the day when the cannon was fired the spectators would number in the millions, for they were already gathering on the narrow peninsula from all over the world. Europe was emigrating to America.

But it must be said that so far the curiosity of these many newcomers had been poorly satisfied. Many of them had counted on seeing the spectacle of the casting, and had seen only its smoke. It was very little for avid eyes, but Barbicane had refused to let anyone watch that operation. And so there was grumbling, dissatisfaction, and complaining. Barbicane was condemned; he was accused of despotism; his conduct was declared un-American. There was almost a riot around the stockade at Stone Hill. Barbicane, as we have seen, remained unshakable in his decision.

But when the cannon had been completely finished, the closed-door policy could no longer be maintained. It would have been ungracious, and even rash, to irritate public feeling. So Barbicane opened the enclosure to one and all. Prompted by his practical mind, however, he decided to make the public's curiosity profitable.

It was a great experience merely to look at the immense cannon, but to descend into its depths was something that every American regarded as the most sublime happiness to be achieved in this world. There was not one visitor who did not want to have the pleasure of seeing that abyss of metal from the inside. Platforms hanging from a steam winch enabled them to satisfy their curiosity. The idea was wildly successful. Women, children, old people, everyone was determined to plumb the mysterious depths of the colossal cannon. The price was five dollars per person, which was by no means cheap, and yet during the two months preceding the experiment the rush of visitors enabled the Gun Club to put half a million dollars into its treasury.

Needless to say, the first men to descend into the cannon were members of the Gun Club, an honor to which the illustrious organization was fully entitled. The solemn ceremony took place on September 25. A cage of honor lowered Barbicane, J. T. Maston, Major Elphiston, General Morgan, Colonel Bloomsberry, Murchison, and other distinguished members of the famous club. There were ten of them in all. It was still quite hot at the bottom of that long metal tube. They all smothered a little. But what joy! What elation! A table set for ten had been placed on the massive stone cube that supported the cannon, whose interior was brightly illuminated by a beam of electric light. Exquisite and numerous dishes, which seemed to descend from the sky, were successively placed on the table, and the finest French wines flowed freely during that magnificent meal served nine hundred feet underground.

The banquet was animated and even noisy. Toasts were proposed right and left. The men drank to the earth, the moon, the Gun Club, the United States, Phoebe, Diana, Selene, and the "peaceful courier of the firmament." All those cheers, borne on the sound waves of the immense acoustic tube, reached its upper end like thunder, and the crowd gathered around Stone Hill cheered in reply, joining in spirit the ten men at the bottom of the cannon.

J. T. Maston was beside himself with joy. It would be difficult to say whether he shouted more than he gesticulated, or whether he drank more than he ate. In any case, he would not have given up his place for an empire—not even, he said, if the cannon were already loaded and primed and about to be fired, sending him into space in little pieces.

CHAPTER 17

A CABLEGRAM

T HE GREAT task undertaken by the Gun Club was, practically speaking, finished, and yet two months still had to go by before the day when the projectile would be sent on its way to the moon. Because of the impatience on all sides, those two months were going to seem as long as two years. So far the newspapers had reported every detail of the operation, and their accounts had been eagerly devoured; but it now seemed likely that this "dividend of interest" distributed to the public was going to be seriously diminished, and everyone was afraid of no longer being able to get his daily ration of excitement.

These fears proved to be groundless. The most unexpected, extraordinary, incredible incident imaginable brought interest to a fever pitch again and threw the whole world into a state of breathless anticipation.

On September 30, at 3:47 P.M., a message that had been sent by means of the Atlantic cable that runs from Valentia, Ireland, to Newfoundland and the American coast was delivered to Barbicane.

He opened the envelope and read the message. Despite his great self-control, when he had read those few words his lips turned pale and his eyes became blurred.

Here is the text of that cablegram, which is now preserved in the archives of the Gun Club:

Paris, France
September 30, 4:00 a.m.
Barbicane
Tampa, Florida, U.S.A..

Replace spherical shell with cylindro-conical one. I will go to moon in it. Am coming on steamer Atlanta.

Michel Ardan

CHAPTER 18

THE PASSENGER ON THE *ATLANTA*

I F, INSTEAD of flashing along electric wires, this stunning message had arrived by ordinary mail and in a sealed envelope, so that a whole series of French, Irish, Newfoundland, and American employees were not necessarily aware of its contents, Barbicane would not have hesitated for a moment. He would have remained silent out of prudence and in order not to cast discredit on his project. The cablegram was perhaps a hoax, especially since it had come from a Frenchman. What likelihood was there that a man could be rash enough even to consider such a trip? And if such a man existed, was he not a lunatic who ought to be put in a padded cell rather than in a projectile?

But the cablegram was known, for the transmission services are not very discreet by nature, and the news of Michel Ardan's proposal was already spreading over the whole country. It would therefore be pointless for Barbicane to remain silent. He called together all his colleagues in Tampa and, without revealing his thoughts or discussing the amount of credence that ought to be given to the cablegram, he calmly read its laconic text.

"Impossible!"

"Incredible!"

"Surely it's a joke!"

"He's only making fun of us!"

"Ridiculous!"

"Absurd!"

For several minutes there were loud expressions of doubt and incredulity, accompanied by the gestures that are customary in such cases. Each man smiled, laughed, or shrugged his shoulders, according to his humor. Only J. T. Maston responded with superb enthusiasm.

"Now *that's* an idea!"

"Yes," said Major Elphiston, "but it's all right to have ideas like that only if you have no intention of carrying them out."

"Why shouldn't it be carried out?" J. T. Maston replied hotly, ready to argue. But none of the others wanted to push him any further.

Meanwhile the name of Michel Ardan was already being repeated in Tampa. Strangers and natives exchanged looks, questioned one another, and made jokes, not about Ardan, who was only a myth, an illusion, but about J. T. Maston for believing in the existence of that fictitious individual. When Barbicane had proposed sending a projectile to the moon, everyone had considered it a natural and practical undertaking, purely a matter of ballistics. But that a sane man should offer to book passage in the projectile, to attempt that fantastic journey—that was a whimsical idea, a joke, a hoax!

The mockery went on till evening without stopping. It can be said that the whole United States was seized with a fit of wild laughter, which is unusual in a country where impossible undertakings readily find advocates, supporters, and backers.

But, like all new ideas, Michel Ardan's proposal bothered certain minds. It had disturbed the course of accustomed emotions. It was something that had not been thought of before. The incident soon became an obsession because of its very strangeness. People thought about it. How many things have been denied one day, only to become realities the next! Why shouldn't someone make a trip to the moon some day? But in any case the man who wanted to risk his life that way must be a madman, and since his plan could not be taken seriously, he would have done better to keep quiet, rather than upsetting a whole country with his ridiculous nonsense.

But first of all, did that man really exist? It was an important question. The name of Michel Ardan was not unknown in America. It belonged to a European who was often cited for his daring feats. And the cablegram sent across the bottom of the Atlantic, the naming of the ship on which the Frenchman had said he was traveling, the date set for its arrival—all these things gave the proposal a certain plausibility. The matter had to be cleared up. Isolated individuals soon formed into groups, the groups were drawn together by curiosity as atoms are drawn together by molecular attraction, and the final result was a compact crowd which moved toward Barbicane's residence.

Since the arrival of the telegram, Barbicane had not declared his opinion. He had let J. T. Maston state his views without expressing either approval or disapproval. His intention was to remain silent and wait for events. But he had reckoned without the impatience of the public. There was a look of dissatisfaction on his face when he saw the population of Tampa gathering beneath his windows. Their vociferous clamor soon forced him to appear. He had all the duties and therefore all the annoyances of fame.

And so he appeared. A hush fell over the crowd, then one citizen spoke up and asked bluntly:

"Is the man called Michel Ardan in the cablegram on his way to America or not?"

"Gentlemen," replied Barbicane, "I don't know any more about it than you do."

"We must find out!" shouted several impatient voices.

"Time will tell," Barbicane said calmly.

"Time has no right to keep a whole country in suspense," said the spokesman. "Have you changed your plans for the projectile, the way the cablegram says?"

"Not yet. But you're right: we must find out. Since the Atlantic cable has caused all this commotion, it's only fair that it should give us more complete information."

"Send a cablegram!" cried the crowd.

Barbicane went down to the street and walked to the telegraph office, followed by the multitude.

A few minutes later, a message was on its way to the ship brokers' central office in Liverpool, asking these questions:

"Is there a ship named the *Atlanta*? Did she recently leave Europe? Does she have a passenger named Michel Ardan?"

Two hours later, Barbicane received an answer whose precision left no room for doubt:

"The steamer *Atlanta,* of Liverpool, left port on October 2, bound for Tampa, with a Frenchman on board listed under the name of Michel Ardan."

When he had read this confirmation of the first cablegram, Barbicane's eyes flashed, his fists clenched violently and he was heard to murmur:

"So it's true! It's possible! That Frenchman exists! And in two weeks he'll be here! But he's a madman, a senseless lunatic! I'll never consent..."

And yet that very evening he wrote to Breadwill &

Co., asking them to postpone casting the projectile until further notice.

To describe the emotion that gripped all America, the way in which the effect of Barbicane's original announcement was surpassed a dozen times, what the American newspapers said, how they accepted the news and trumpeted the arrival of that hero from the Old World, the feverish agitation in which everyone lived, counting the hours, minutes, and seconds; to give even a faint idea of the exhausting obsession of all those minds dominated by a single thought; to show all occupations yielding to one preoccupation, work stopped, business suspended, ships ready to put to sea remaining tied up in port in order not to miss the arrival of the *Atlanta,* trains arriving full and leaving empty, Tampa Bay constantly being crossed by steamers, packet boats, yachts, and flyboats of all sizes; to enumerate the thousands of people who quadrupled the population of Tampa in two weeks and had to camp in tents like an army in the field—all that would be a task beyond human strength, and could not be undertaken without foolhardiness.

On October 20, at nine o'clock in the morning, signal stations on the Straits of Florida reported thick smoke on the horizon. Two hours later, a big steamer exchanged recognition signals with them. The name of the *Atlanta* was immediately sent to Tampa. At four o'clock the English ship entered Tampa Bay. At five she steamed into the channel at full speed. At six she dropped anchor in the port of Tampa.

Before the anchor had bitten into the sandy bottom, the *Atlanta* was surrounded by five hundred boats and taken by storm. Barbicane was the first to step on board. He cried out in a voice whose emotion he tried to control:

"Michel Ardan!"

"Present!" replied a man standing on the poop deck.

With crossed arms, questioning eyes, and sealed lips, Barbicane scrutinized the *Atlanta*'s passenger.

He was a man of forty-two, tall but already a little round-shouldered, like those caryatids that hold balconies on their backs. He had a strong, leonine head, and he occasionally shook his mane of fiery hair. A short face, broad at the temples, a mustache that bristled like a cat's whiskers, cheeks adorned with little tufts of yellowish hair, and round, distracted, rather nearsighted eyes completed that eminently feline physiognomy. But his nose was boldly drawn, his mouth was particularly humane, his forehead was high, intelligent, and furrowed like a field that never lies fallow. Finally, his well-developed torso firmly planted on a pair of long legs, his powerful, muscular arms, and his resolute bearing made him a vigorous, solidly built man, "forged rather than cast," to borrow a phrase from the metallurgical art.

Disciples of Lavater or Gratiolet would easily have seen on his skull and face the incontestable signs of combativeness, that is, courage in danger and a tendency to break down obstacles. They would also have seen signs of kindness and a highly developed imagination, a faculty which inclines certain temperaments to have a passion for superhuman things. But the bumps of acquisitiveness, the need to possess and acquire, were totally lacking.

To finish describing his physical appearance, we must mention his loose, comfortable clothes, his shirt collar generously opened on his robust neck, and his invariably unbuttoned cuffs, from which his restless hands emerged. He gave the impression that, even in the middle of winter or at the peak of danger, he was never cold, and that he particularly never had cold feet.

On the deck of the steamer, in the midst of the crowd,

he paced back and forth, never staying in one place, "dragging his anchor," as the sailors said, gesticulating, speaking familiarly to everyone, and biting his nails with nervous avidity. He was one of those originals whom the Creator invents in a moment of whimsy, then immediately breaks the mold.

Michel Ardan's personality offered a broad field to observation and analysis. He was unfailingly inclined to exaggeration and had not yet passed the age of superlatives. Objects were registered on his retina with inordinate dimensions, and this led to his associations of gigantic ideas. He saw everything bigger than natural, except difficulties and men.

He had a luxuriant nature; he was an artist by instinct, and a witty man who used sniper tactics rather than keeping up a running fire of clever remarks. In a discussion he cared little for logic and was hostile to the syllogism, which he would never have invented, but he had his own methods of attack. He was a master of the deadly *ad hominem* argument, and he liked to defend hopeless causes tooth and claw.

Among other idiosyncrasies, he proclaimed himself to be "sublimely ignorant," like Shakespeare, and he professed to despise scientists and scholars, who were, he said, "people who do nothing but keep score while we play the game." He was a Bohemian from Wonderland, adventurous but not an adventurer, a daredevil, a Phaëthon driving the sun chariot at breakneck speed; an Icarus with spare wings. He never shrank from personal risk, he threw himself into insane ventures with his eyes wide open, he burned his ships behind him with more enthusiasm than Agathocles, and, ready to break his neck at any time, he invariably landed on his feet, like those little wooden acrobats that children play with.

In two words, his motto was "Even so!" and love of the impossible was his ruling passion, to use Pope's excellent expression.

But he also had the defects that went with his good qualities. Nothing ventured, nothing gained; he ventured often, but he still had little. He was a spendthrift, a wastrel. He was completely unselfish and obeyed his heart as often as he did his head. Obliging and chivalrous, he would not have signed the death warrant of his cruelest enemy, and he would have sold himself into slavery in order to free a slave.

In France and all over Europe, everyone knew that sparkling, noisy man. The hundred voices of fame had talked themselves hoarse about him. He lived in a glass house and confided his most intimate secrets to the whole world. He also had an admirable collection of enemies among those whom he had jostled, bruised, or mercilessly knocked down as he elbowed his way through the crowd.

Generally, however, he was liked and treated as a spoiled child. He had to be taken as he was or not at all, and he was taken. Everyone was interested in his bold ventures and watched him with concern. He was so recklessly daring! Whenever a friend tried to stop him by predicting imminent catastrophe, he would smile graciously and answer, "The forest is burned only by its own trees," without realizing that he was quoting the prettiest of all Arab proverbs.

Such was Michel Ardan as he stood on the deck of the *Atlanta,* always agitated, always boiling from the heat of an inner fire, deeply excited, not about what he had come to do in America—he was not even thinking about it— but simply because of his feverish nervous system. If ever two men presented a striking contrast, it was the Frenchman Michel Ardan and the American Barbicane, though each was enterprising, bold, and daring in his manner.

Barbicane's contemplation of that rival who had just thrust him into the background was interrupted by the cheers of the crowd. Their shouting became so frenzied, and their enthusiasm took such personal forms, that Michel Ardan, after having shaken a thousand hands at the risk of losing all his fingers, had to take refuge in his cabin.

Barbicane accompanied him without having said a word.

"You're Barbicane?" Ardan asked as soon as they were alone together. His tone was the same as he would have used in speaking to a friend he had known for twenty years.

"Yes."

"Then hello, Barbicane! How are you?"

"Are you determined to go through with it?" Barbicane asked without wasting time on preliminaries.

"Absolutely determined."

"Nothing will make you change your mind?"

"Nothing. Have you altered your projectile the way I asked you to in my cablegram?"

"I was waiting for you to come...But tell me," Barbicane said insistently, "have you thought it over carefully?"

"Thought it over? I can't waste time on that. I've found a chance to visit the moon, I'm going to take it, and that's all there is to it. I see no reason why I should think it over."

Barbicane stared avidly at that man who spoke of his planned trip to the moon so lightly and casually, and with such a complete lack of anxiety.

"But you must at least have some definite plan in mind," he said.

"Yes, I have an excellent plan. But if you don't mind, I'd rather tell my story once and for all, to everyone, and never go into it again. That way, I won't have to repeat myself. So let me ask you to summon your friends, your colleagues, the whole town, the whole state, the whole country if you like, and tomorrow I'll be ready to describe my plan and answer any objections that may be raised. Don't worry: I'll be waiting for them with confidence. Does that suit you?"

"It does," replied Barbicane.

He left the cabin and told the crowd about Ardan's suggestion. His words were received with a joyous uproar. The arrangement would cut short all difficulty. The next day, everyone would be able to examine the European hero at leisure. Some of the more stubborn onlookers, however, refused to leave the deck of the *Atlanta* and spent the night on board. Among them was J. T. Maston, who had screwed his hook into the poop rail; it would have taken a winch to pull him loose.

"He's a hero! A hero!" he shouted fervently. "We're nothing but a bunch of old women compared to him!"

As for Barbicane, after having asked the visitors to leave he went back into Ardan's cabin and stayed there till the ship's bell struck midnight.

Then the two rivals in popularity warmly shook hands and Ardan bade Barbicane an affectionate good night.

CHAPTER 19

A MEETING

THE NEXT day the sun rose too late to suit the impatient public. They felt it was behaving sluggishly for a sun that was to illuminate such a great occasion. Fearing that Michel Ardan might be asked indiscreet questions, Barbicane would have liked him to limit the audience to a small number of informed people, to his colleagues, for example. It would have been easier to dam up Niagara Falls. He had to give up the idea and let his new friend run the risks of a public appearance. The main room of Tampa's new stock exchange building was judged insufficient despite its colossal size, for the planned assembly was taking on the proportions of a mass meeting.

The place chosen was a vast plain outside the town. Within a few hours it was sheltered from the rays of the sun: the ships in the harbor, rich in sails, rigging, spare masts and yards, supplied the material for a gigantic tent. A canvas sky soon stretched over the baked earth and defended it against the attacks of the sun. Three hundred thousand people gathered under it and braved the stifling heat for several hours, waiting for the Frenchman to arrive. A third of the crowd could see and hear, another third could see little and hear nothing, and the final third could neither see nor hear, though they were no less eager to applaud.

At three o'clock Michel Ardan made his appearance, accompanied by the principal members of the Gun Club. On his right was Barbicane, and on his left was J. T. Maston, more radiant than the noonday sun. Ardan mounted the platform, from where he looked out over an ocean of black hats. He seemed quite relaxed and not at all embarrassed; he was gay, familiar, and amiable, as though he felt perfectly at home. He bowed gracefully to the cheers that greeted him. Then, after raising his hand to ask for silence, he began speaking in admirably correct English:

"Gentlemen, although it's very hot I'm going to take up some of your time to tell you a few things about my plans, which apparently interest you. I'm neither an orator nor a scientist, and I wasn't expecting to speak in public, but my friend Barbicane told me it would please you, so I'm glad to do it. Listen to me with your six hundred thousand ears and please excuse any mistakes I may make."

The crowd liked this straightforward beginning. They expressed their appreciation by an immense murmur of satisfaction.

"Feel free to express your approval or disapproval in any way," he went on. "First of all, you must bear in mind that you're dealing with an ignorant man. But my ignorance is so vast that I'm even ignorant of difficulties. So it seemed to me a simple, natural, and easy matter to reserve passage in a projectile and go to the moon. It's a trip that has to be made sooner or later. As for the means of making it, it simply follows the law of progress. Man began by traveling on all fours, then on two feet, then in a cart, then in a wagon, then in a carriage, then in a railroad car. And the vehicle of the future is the projectile. The planets themselves are merely projectiles, cannon balls set in motion by the hand of the Creator. But let's come back to our vehicle. Some of you, gentlemen, may feel that the speed which will be given to it is excessive. That's by no means true. All the heavenly bodies move faster. The earth is now carrying us three times as fast in its motion around the sun.

"Let me give you the speeds at which the various planets move. I must admit that, despite my ignorance, I know that little astronomical detail quite well; but within two minutes you'll be as learned on the subject as I am. Neptune moves at the rate of 12,500 miles an hour; Uranus at 17,500; Saturn at 22,145; Jupiter at 29,190; Mars at 55,030; Earth at 68,750; Venus at 80,080; and Mercury at 131,300. Some comets have a velocity of 3,500,000 miles an hour at their perihelion! As for us in our projectile, we'll be loafing along at a leisurely pace of only 24,400 miles an hour at the beginning, and our speed will be constantly decreasing! Is that anything to be excited about? Isn't it obvious that all this will be surpassed some day by still greater speeds, whose mechanical agents will probably be light or electricity?"

No one seemed to have any doubt about the matter.

"If we're to believe certain narrow-minded people—I don't know what else to call them—mankind is enclosed in a circle from which there's no escape, and doomed to vegetate on this globe without ever being able to soar into interplanetary space! It's not true! We're about to go to the moon, and someday we'll go to the planets or the stars as easily and quickly as we now go from New York to Liverpool! The oceans of space will soon be crossed as the oceans of the earth are crossed today! Distance is only a relative term, and it will eventually be reduced to zero."

Though strongly inclined in favor of the French hero,

the crowd was a little taken aback by this daring theory. Ardan apparently sensed their reaction.

"You don't seem convinced," he said with a charming smile. "Well, let's reason a little. Do you know how long it would take an express train to reach the moon? Three hundred days. That's all. The distance is 214,000 miles, but what does that amount to? It's less than nine times the circumference of the earth, and there's no experienced sailor or traveler who hasn't covered more distance than that in his life. Think of it: my trip will take only ninety-seven hours! You may think that the moon is far away and that a man ought to think twice before trying to go there, but what would you say if it were a question of going to Neptune, which moves in an orbit 2,867,500,000 miles from the sun! There's a trip that not many people could afford to make, even if it cost only a dime a mile! Baron Rothschild himself, with his $200,000,000, would be $86,750,000 short of having enough to pay his fare, and would have to stay behind!"

This line of reasoning seemed to please the crowd greatly. Full of his subject, Michel Ardan threw himself into it with superb gusto; feeling that he was being avidly listened to, he continued with admirable self-assurance:

"Well, my friends, the distance from Neptune to the sun is nothing at all compared to the distances from here to the stars. To express those distances, we must enter that awesome realm where the smallest numbers have ten digits, and take the billion as our unit. Excuse me for being so well up on this subject, but it's fascinating. Listen and judge for yourselves. Alpha Centauri is 20,000 billion miles away; Sirius 125,000 billion; Arcturus 130,000 billion; Polaris 292,000 billion; Capella 425,000 billion; and other stars are thousands, millions, and billions of billions of miles away! How can anyone even consider the wretched little distances that separate the planets from the sun? How can anyone even maintain that they exist? What an error! What an aberration of the senses! Do you know what I think of the world that begins with the sun and ends with Neptune? Would you like to know my theory? It's quite simple. To me, the solar system is a solid, homogenous body; the planets that compose it touch, press against, and adhere to one another, and the space between them is only the space that separates the molecules of the most compact metals, such as silver, iron, gold, or platinum. I therefore have a right to maintain, and I repeat it with a conviction that will be communicated to all of you: 'Distance' is an empty word, distance does not exist!"

"Well said! Bravo! Hurrah!" cried the audience, electrified by his gestures, his tone, and the boldness of his concepts.

"No," J. T. Maston said more forcefully than the others, "distance doesn't exist!"

Carried away by the violence of his movements, by the impetus of his body, which he was scarcely able to control, he nearly fell off the platform. But he succeeded in catching his balance, thus avoiding a fall which would have brusquely proved to him that distance was not an empty word. Then the stirring speech continued:

"My friends, I think that question is settled now. If I haven't convinced all of you, it's because I've been timid in my demonstrations and weak in my arguments, and you'll have to blame the insufficiency of my theoretical studies. Be that as it may, I repeat that the distance from the earth to the moon is truly unimportant and unworthy of preoccupying a serious mind. I don't think I'm going too far in saying that in the near future there will be trains of projectiles in which one can travel comfortably from the earth to the moon. There will be neither collisions nor derailments to fear, and the passengers will reach their destination rapidly, without fatigue, in a straight line—as the crow flies, so to speak. Within twenty years, half the people on earth will have visited the moon!"

"Hurray! Hurrah for Michel Ardan!" cried his listeners, even the least convinced.

"Hurrah for Barbicane!" he replied modestly.

This expression of gratitude toward the promoter of the enterprise was greeted with unanimous applause.

"And now, my friends," he said, "if you have any questions to ask, you'll embarrass a poor man like me, of course, but I'll try to answer them nevertheless."

So far Barbicane had every reason to be satisfied with the direction the discussion had taken. It had dealt with speculative theories, in which Michel Ardan, carried along by his lively imagination, had made a brilliant impression. Barbicane felt he must prevent it from turning to practical matters because Ardan would probably make a much poorer showing in them. He hastened to ask him if he thought the moon or the planets were inhabited.

"You've just asked me a big question," Ardan replied, smiling. "However, if I'm not mistaken, men of great intelligence, such as Plutarch, Swedenborg, Bernardin de Saint-Pierre, and many others, have answered it in the affirmative. Looking at it from the viewpoint of natural history, I'd be inclined to agree with them; I'd tell myself that nothing useless exists in this world, and, answering your question by raising another, I'd say that if those worlds are inhabitable, they either are, have been, or will be inhabited."

"You're right!" shouted the first row of spectators, whose opinion had the force of law for the last ones.

"No one could give a more logical or precise answer,"

said Barbicane. "The question comes down to this: Are the worlds inhabitable. For my part, I believe they are."

"And I'm certain of it," said Ardan.

"But there are arguments against it," said one of the spectators. "Most of the principles of life would have to be modified. On the planets, for example, it must be either burning hot or fantastically cold, depending on how far they are from the sun."

"I'm sorry I don't know my honorable contradictor personally," said Ardan, "because I'd try to answer him if I did. His objection has a certain validity, but I think that it and all other objections to the inhabitability of other worlds can be countered rather successfully. If I were a physicist I'd say that if less heat is set in motion on planets near the sun, and more on those farther away, that is enough to balance the temperatures of the planets and make them bearable for beings like us. If I were a naturalist, I'd say, in agreement with many famous scientists, that nature on our own earth gives us examples of animals living in greatly diversified conditions of inhabitability: fish breathe in a medium that's lethal to other animals; amphibians have a double life that's rather difficult to explain; deep-sea creatures live under pressures of fifty or sixty atmospheres without being crushed; certain aquatic insects, insensitive to temperature, are found in springs of boiling hot water as well as in polar seas; and finally I'd say that we must recognize in nature a diversity in her means of action which is often incomprehensible but none the less real, and which borders on omnipotence. If I were a chemist, I'd say that meteorites, which were obviously formed outside our terrestrial world, have shown undeniable traces of carbon, that this substance owes its origin only to living organisms, and that, according to Reichenbach's experiments, it must necessarily have been 'animalized.' If I were a theologian, I'd say that, according to Saint Paul, divine redemption seems to have been applied not only to earth but to all celestial worlds. But I'm not a theologian, a chemist, a naturalist, or a physicist, so in my total ignorance of the great laws that govern the universe I'll limit myself to this answer: I don't know if other worlds are inhabited, and since I don't know, I'll go there to find out!"

Did the opponent of Ardan's theories venture other arguments? It is impossible to say, for the frenzied shouts of the crowd would have prevented any opinion from being heard. When silence had returned to even the furthest groups, the triumphant orator added these final considerations:

"As I'm sure you realize, my friends, I've done no more than scratch the surface of this great question. I'm not here to teach you a course or defend a thesis on it. There's a whole series of other arguments in favor of the inhabitability of other worlds. I won't even mention them. Allow me to stress only one point. If someone maintains that the planets are uninhabited, he may be answered as follows: 'You may be right, if it can be proved that the earth is the best of all possible worlds. But that's not the case, no matter what Voltaire's Dr. Pangloss may have said. The earth has only one satellite, whereas Jupiter, Uranus, Saturn, and Neptune have several in their service, an advantage that's not to be scorned. But the main thing that makes our globe uncomfortable is the inclination of its axis in relation to the plane of its orbit. That's what causes the inequality of our days and nights, and the unfortunate diversity of our seasons. On our wretched spheroid it's always either too hot or too cold. We freeze in winter and swelter in summer. Ours is the planet of colds, pneumonia, and consumption, while on the surface of Jupiter, for example, whose axis has little inclination,* the inhabitants can enjoy unvarying temperatures. There are permanent zones of spring, summer, fall, and winter. Each Jovian can choose the climate he likes and spend his whole life in freedom from variations of temperatures. You'll have to admit that that's one way in which Jupiter is superior to the earth, not to mention the fact that its years are twelve years long! Furthermore, it's obvious to me that, living under such marvelous conditions, the inhabitants of that fortunate world are superior beings, that their scholars are more scholarly, their artists more artistic, their bad people less bad, and their good people better. And what does our globe lack in order to attain that perfection? Very little! Only an axis of rotation less inclined with respect to the plane of its orbit."

"Well, then," cried an impetuous voice, "let's unite our efforts, invent machines, and straighten the earth's axis!"

A thunder of applause greeted this bold proposal, whose author was and could only have been J. T. Maston. His engineering instincts probably led him to make it without reflecting, but it must be said, for it is true, that many of the spectators backed him with their shouts, and if they had had the point of support requested by Archimedes, the Americans would no doubt have constructed a lever capable of moving the earth and straightening its axis. But a point of support was precisely what those daring mechanics lacked.

Nevertheless this "eminently practical" idea was enormously successful. The discussion was suspended for a good quarter of an hour, and for a long time afterward people all over the United States talked of the plan so forcefully put forward by the secretary of the Gun Club.

*Only 3° 5'.

CHAPTER 20

THRUST AND COUNTERTHRUST

IT SEEMED for a long time that this incident was going to put an end to the discussion. No one could have thought of a better way to climax it. But when the agitation had died down, these words were spoken in a loud, stern voice:

"Now that the speaker has given free rein to his imagination, will he please return to his subject, do less theorizing and discuss the practical aspects of his expedition?"

All eyes turned to the man who had just spoken. He was hard and gaunt, with an energetic face and an American-style beard growing abundantly under his chin. Taking advantage of the various waves of agitation that had gone through the audience, he had made his way to the front row. There, with his arms crossed and his eyes shining boldly, he was staring imperturbably at the hero of the meeting. After having asked his question, he fell silent and was apparently affected by neither the thousands of gazes converging on him nor the murmur of disapproval stirred up by his words. When an answer was not forthcoming, he asked his question again with the same sharp, precise intonation, then he added:

"We're here to deal with the moon, not with the earth."

"You're right," replied Michel Ardan, "the discussion has wandered. Let's come back to the moon."

"Mr. Ardan," said the stranger, "you claim that the moon is inhabited. Maybe so, but one thing is sure: if there are any people up there, they live without breathing, because—I'm giving you this warning for your own good— there isn't one single molecule of air on the moon's surface."

When he heard this, Ardan shook his tawny mane; he realized that this man was turning the discussion to the heart of the matter. He stared back at him and said:

"So there's no air on the moon! Would you mind telling me who says so?"

"Scientists."

"Really?"

"Really."

"Sir," said Ardan, "all joking aside, I have deep respect for scientists who know, but deep disdain for those who don't."

"Do you know any who belong in that latter category?"

"Yes. In France there's one who maintains that, 'mathematically,' birds can't fly, and there's another one whose theories demonstrate that fish aren't made to live in water."

"I'm not concerned with them, Mr. Ardan. To support what I'm saying, I could cite names that you wouldn't reject."

"I'd be highly embarrassed if you did, sir. I'm an ignorant man and I ask nothing better than to learn."

"Then why do you deal with scientific matters if you haven't studied them?" the stranger asked rather bluntly.

"Why? Because a man is always brave if he's unaware of danger! I know nothing, it's true, but my weakness is precisely what makes my strength."

"Your weakness goes to the point of madness!" the stranger said irritably.

"If my madness takes me to the moon, so much the better!"

Barbicane and his colleagues had been scrutinizing the intruder who was trying so audaciously to thwart Ardan's plan. None of them knew him. Uncertain about the results of such a frank discussion, Barbicane looked at Ardan with a certain apprehension. The spectators were attentive and seriously concerned, for the dispute was calling their attention to the dangers or perhaps even the impossibilities of the expedition.

"The arguments against the existence of an atmosphere on the moon are numerous and unassailable," said the stranger. "First of all, I can say that if the moon ever did have an atmosphere, it was necessarily drawn away from it by the earth. But I prefer to confront you with undeniable facts."

"Please do," Ardan replied gallantly. "Confront me with as many of them as you like."

"As you know," said the stranger, "when light rays pass through a medium such as air they're deflected from a straight line; in other words, they undergo refraction. Now when stars are occulted by the moon, the light from them never shows the slightest deviation or gives any sign of refraction when it passes by the moon's edge. This clearly means that the moon has no atmosphere."

Everyone looked at Ardan, for if he granted the point its consequences would be obvious.

"That's your best argument," he replied, "not to say your only one, and a scientist might be at a loss to answer it. As for me, I'll say only that it isn't absolutely conclusive because it presupposes that the angular diameter of the moon has been perfectly determined, which it hasn't.

But let's not dwell on that. Tell me, do you admit the existence of volcanoes on the moon?"

"Extinct ones, yes; active ones, no."

"Even so, it certainly isn't illogical to assume that those volcanoes were active at some time in the past, is it?"

"Of course not, but since they themselves could have supplied the oxygen necessary for combustion, the fact of their eruption doesn't prove the presence of an atmosphere."

"Then let's go on," said Ardan, "and leave that kind of argument in favor of direct observation. But I warn you that I'm going to mention names."

"Go ahead and mention them."

"I will. In 1715 when the astronomers Louville and Halley were observing the eclipse of May 3, they noticed some strange, rapid flashes that were repeated often. They attributed them to storms raging in the moon's atmosphere."

"In 1715," said the stranger, "the astronomers Louville and Halley mistook purely terrestrial phenomena taking place in the earth's atmosphere, such as meteorites, for lunar phenomena. That's what scientists answered when they first made their announcement, and I make the same answer."

"Let's go on," said Ardan, undisturbed. "Isn't it true that in 1787 Herschel observed many points of light on the surface of the moon?"

"Yes, but he didn't try to explain them and he didn't conclude that they indicated the existence of a lunar atmosphere."

"That was an excellent answer," said Ardan, complimenting his adversary. "I see that your knowledge of the moon is very great."

"Yes, it is, and I'll add that the most skillful observers, those who have studied the moon more than anyone else, namely, Beer and Moelder, agree in maintaining that it has no atmosphere whatever."

The crowd stirred, apparently deeply affected by the stranger's arguments.

"Let's still go on," Ardan said with great calm, "and now let's come to an important fact. When he was observing the solar eclipse of July 18, 1860, Laussedat, an able French astronomer, noted that the points of the sun's crescent were blunted and rounded. It was a phenomenon that could have been produced only by the deviation of the sun's rays passing through the moon's atmosphere. There's no other possible explanation."

"But is the fact certain?" the stranger asked sharply.

"Absolutely certain!"

The crowd stirred again, this time with a surge of renewed confidence in its hero. His adversary remained silent. Without gloating over his advantage, Ardan said simply:

"You can see, sir, that we mustn't rule out the possibility of an atmosphere on the moon. It's probably quite rarefied, but nowadays science generally grants that it exists."

"Not on the mountains, with all due respect to your learning," said the stranger, reluctant to back down.

"No, but it exists in the valleys, though it doesn't go higher than a few hundred feet."

"In any case, you'll do well to take precautions, because that air will be terribly thin."

"Oh, there'll surely be enough for one man! Besides, once I'm up there I'll try to economize by breathing only on great occasions."

A formidable burst of laughter thundered in the mysterious stranger's ears. He looked over the crowd with proud defiance.

"Since we agree on the presence of a certain amount of air," Ardan went on cheerfully, "we're forced to admit the presence of a certain amount of water. It's a conclusion I'm glad to draw, for my own sake. And let me point out something else to you: we know only one side of the moon, and while there's probably not much air on the side facing us, it's possible that there's a lot of it on the other side."

"Why?"

"Because the pull of the earth's gravity has made the moon take the shape of an egg with its small end toward us. This means, according to Hansen's calculations, that its center of gravity is in the other hemisphere, and so we can conclude that all its air and water must have been drawn to its other side from the first days of its creation."

"Pure fantasy!" cried the stranger.

"No, it's pure theory based on the laws of mechanics, and I think it would be hard to refute it. I appeal to this assembly. Let's put the question to a vote: Is life, as it exists on earth, possible on the moon?"

Three hundred thousand people voiced their affirmation. The stranger tried to speak, but was unable to make himself heard. He was deluged with shouts and threats:

"Enough! Enough!"

"Get out, you intruder!"

"Throw him out!"

But, firmly gripping the platform, he stood his ground and let the storm pass. It would have taken on alarming proportions if Michel Ardan had not quelled it with a gesture. He was too chivalrous to abandon his adversary in such a predicament.

"Would you like to add a few words?" he asked graciously.

"Yes, a hundred, a thousand!" the stranger replied heatedly. "Or rather no, only a few. To persist in your plan, you must be . . ."

"Imprudent? How can you call me that when I've asked my friend Barbicane for a cylindro-conical shell so I won't spin around like a squirrel in a cage?"

"But, you poor fool, the terrible jolt will smash you flat as soon as you start!"

"You've just put your finger on the only real difficulty! However, I have too high an opinion of American industrial genius not to believe that it won't be resolved."

"But what about the heat developed by the projectile as it passes through the air?"

"Its walls will be thick, and it will take so little time to get through the earth's atmosphere!"

"What about food and water?"

"I've calculated that I can take along enough for a year, and my journey will last only four days!"

"And what about air?"

"I'll make it by chemical processes."

"And your fall on the moon, assuming you ever get there?"

"It will be only a sixth as fast as a fall on the earth, since the pull of gravity is only a sixth as strong on the moon."

"But it will still be enough to break you like a glass!"

"What's to stop me from slowing down my fall by igniting properly placed rockets at the right time?"

"All right, suppose we say all those difficulties are resolved, all those obstacles are overcome; suppose we put all the chances in your favor and say you arrive safe and sound on the moon. How will you get back?"

"I won't."

At this reply, which reached the sublime by its simplicity, the crowd remained silent. But its silence was more eloquent than its shouts of enthusiasm would have been. The stranger took advantage of it to protest one last time:

"You're sure to be killed, and your senseless death won't even have served science!"

"Go on," said Ardan, "continue with your pleasant predictions!"

"This is too much! I don't know why I go on with such a ridiculous discussion! Persist in your insane plan if you want to! You're not the one who's to blame!"

"Don't be afraid of offending me!"

"No, another man will bear the responsibility of your acts!"

"Who is that man?" Ardan asked imperiously.

"The man who organized this whole absurd, impossible project!"

This was a direct attack. Ever since the stranger's intervention, Barbicane had been making violent efforts to control himself and "burn his smoke," as certain boiler furnaces do, but when he heard himself referred to so outrageously he leapt to his feet. He was about to walk over to the adversary who was staring defiantly at him when he was suddenly separated from him.

The platform was abruptly picked up by a hundred vigorous arms and Barbicane had to share the honors of triumph with Michel Ardan. The platform was heavy, but the bearers were constantly relieved because each man was arguing, struggling, and fighting for the privilege of giving the demonstration the support of his shoulders.

Meanwhile the stranger had not taken advantage of the tumult to leave. Would he have been able to make his way through that dense crowd? Probably not. In any case, he stood in the front row, with his arms crossed, looking intently at Barbicane.

Barbicane never lost sight of him. The two men's gazes remained engaged like two quivering swords.

The shouting of the immense crowd continued unabated all through that triumphal march. Michel Ardan was obviously enjoying it. His face was radiant. Now and then the platform seemed to pitch and roll like a ship in a storm, but the two heroes of the meeting had their sea legs; they never faltered, and their ship safely reached port in Tampa. Michel Ardan fortunately succeeded in escaping the last embraces of his robust admirers. He fled to the Hotel Franklin, hurried up to his room, and quickly slipped into bed while an army of a hundred thousand men kept watch under his windows.

During this time a short, grave, and decisive scene took place between the mysterious stranger and Barbicane.

Free at last, Barbicane went straight up to his adversary.

"Come," he said curtly.

The stranger followed him to the waterfront and they were soon alone at the entrance to a wharf. There the two enemies looked at each other.

"Who are you?" asked Barbicane.

"Captain Nicholl."

"I thought so. Till now our paths hadn't crossed..."

"I've deliberately crossed yours!"

"You've insulted me!"

"Yes, publicly."

"And you're going to give me satisfaction for that insult."

"Immediately."

"No. I want everything to take place secretly between

us. There's a forest known as the Skersnaw Woods, three miles outside of Tampa. Do you know where it is?"

"Yes."

"Are you willing to walk into one side of it tomorrow morning at five o'clock?"

"Yes, if you'll walk into the other side of it at the same time."

"And you won't forget your rifle, will you?" asked Barbicane.

"No, and I'm sure you won't forget yours," replied Nicholl.

With these coldly spoken words, the two men parted. Barbicane went home, but instead of getting a few hours' sleep he spent the night trying to think of a way to soften the initial jolt inside the projectile and solve the difficult problem raised by Michel Ardan during the discussion at the meeting.

CHAPTER 21

HOW A FRENCHMAN SETTLES A QUARREL

WHILE THE conditions of this duel—a terrible, savage kind of duel in which each adversary becomes a manhunter—were being discussed by Barbicane and Nicholl, Michel Ardan was resting from the fatigue of his triumph. "Resting" is not a very accurate word, because American beds can rival any marble or granite tabletop for hardness.

Ardan was sleeping rather badly, tossing and turning between the napkins that served as his sheets. He was dreaming of installing a more comfortable bed in his projectile when a violent noise awakened him. His door was being shaken by disorderly blows, apparently struck with some sort of metal instrument. Loud shouting was mingled with this early morning uproar.

"Open your door!" cried a voice. "In the name of heaven, open your door!"

Ardan had no reason to grant such a loudly stated request. However, he got up and opened the door just as it was about to yield to the efforts of his obstinate visitor. J. T. Maston burst into the room. An artillery shell could not have entered with less ceremony.

"Yesterday Barbicane was publicly insulted at the meeting," he said abruptly. "He challenged his adversary, who's none other than Captain Nicholl! They're fighting this morning in the Skersnaw Woods! I learned about it from Barbicane himself. If he's killed, it will mean the end of our project. The duel mustn't be fought! There's only one man with enough influence over Barbicane to make him stop, and that man is Michel Ardan!"

While J. T. Maston was speaking, Ardan, realizing the futility of trying to interrupt him, had quickly pulled on his loose trousers. Less than two minutes later, the two men were hurrying toward the outskirts of Tampa.

On the way J. T. Maston told Ardan the details of the situation. He explained the real causes of the enmity between Barbicane and Nicholl, how it had existed for a long time, and why till now, thanks to mutual friends, the two rivals had never met face to face. He added that it was entirely a matter of rivalry between armor plate and projectiles, and that the scene at the meeting had been only an opportunity to satisfy his rancor which Nicholl had been seeking for a long time.

Nothing could be more terrible than those duels peculiar to America, in which each adversary looks for the other in the woods, lies in wait for him and tries to shoot him down like a wild animal. Each of them must envy the wonderful qualities so natural to the Indians: their quick intelligence, their craftiness, their tracking skill, their ability to sense the presence of an enemy. A mistake, a hesitation, or a misstep can bring death. During these duels the adversaries are often accompanied by their dogs, and, hunters and hunted at the same time, they pursue each other for hours on end.

"What devilish people are you!" Ardan exclaimed when J. T. Maston had given him a description of the whole procedure.

"That's how we are," J. T. Maston replied modestly. "But let's hurry."

Although he and Ardan ran across rice fields and dewy meadows, forded creeks and took every shortcut they could, they were not able to reach the Skersnaw Woods until half past five. Barbicane was to have entered it half an hour earlier.

They soon saw a backwoodsman chopping firewood. J. T. Maston ran up to him, shouting:

"Have you seen a man with a rifle come into the woods? It's Barbicane, the president of the Gun Club, my best friend!"

He naively assumed that Barbicane was known to everyone in the world. But the backwoodsman did not seem to understand.

"A hunter," said Ardan.

"A hunter? Yes, I saw one."

"How long ago?"

"About an hour."

"Too late!" cried J. T. Maston.

"And have you heard any shots?" asked Ardan.

"No."

"Not a single one?"

"Not a single one. Your hunter doesn't seem to be having good hunting!"

"What shall we do?" asked J. T. Maston.

"Go on into the woods," replied Ardan, "at the risk of getting a bullet that's not meant for us."

"Ah," cried J. T. Maston in a tone that left no room for doubt, "I'd rather have ten bullets in my head than one in Barbicane's!"

"Then let's go!" said Ardan, pressing J. T. Maston's hand.

A few seconds later the two friends disappeared into the woods. It was a thick forest made of cypresses, sycamores, tulip trees, olive trees, tamarinds, live oaks, and magnolias. The branches of all these trees were mingled in a dense tangle that made it impossible to see very far. Ardan and J. T. Maston walked side by side, passing through vigorous vines, peering into the bushes hidden in the heavy shadows of the foliage, and expecting to hear a rifle shot at every step. They were unable to recognize any of the traces that Barbicane must have left as he passed; they walked blindly along the almost invisible trails, on which an Indian would have been able to follow an adversary step by step.

After an hour of unsuccessful searching, they stopped. Their apprehension redoubled.

"It must be all over," J. T. Maston said, discouraged. "A man like Barbicane wouldn't have tried to trap his enemy or use any kind of trickery with him. He's too straightforward, too brave. He must have gone straight ahead, into the teeth of danger, and he must have gone so far that the man we talked to wasn't able to hear the shot."

"Surely *we* would have heard a shot in all the time we've been in the woods!"

"But what if we came too late?" J. T. Maston said in despair.

Ardan could think of no reply. They began walking again. Now and then they loudly called either Barbicane or Nicholl, but neither of them answered. Joyful flocks of birds, roused by the noise, vanished between the branches, and a few frightened deer ran off into the thickets.

They searched for another hour. They had already explored most of the forest. There was no trace of either Barbicane or Nicholl. They were beginning to doubt what the backwoodsman had told them, and Ardan was about to give up the futile search, when J. T. Maston stopped abruptly.

"Sh! I see someone!"

"Someone?"

"Yes, a man. He's not moving. He's not holding his rifle. What can he be doing?"

"Do you recognize him?" asked Ardan, whose nearsighted eyes were of little use in such circumstances.

"Yes! He's turning around!"

"Who is it?"

"It's Captain Nicholl!"

"Nicholl!" exclaimed Ardan. He felt his heart contract violently. Nicholl was unarmed—it must mean that he had nothing more to fear from his adversary! "Let's go to him and find out what's happened."

But before they had taken fifty steps they stopped to examine the captain more attentively. They had expected to see a bloodthirsty man absorbed in vengeance; they were dumbfounded at what they saw.

A tight net was stretched between two gigantic tulip trees, and in the middle of it was a little bird with its wings entangled, struggling and crying out plaintively. The net had been placed there not by a human being, but by a venomous spider peculiar to the region, with enormous legs and a body the size of a pigeon's egg. Just as it was about to seize its prey the hideous animal had scurried away and sought refuge in the high branches of a tree, because a formidable enemy had appeared.

Captain Nicholl had laid his rifle on the ground, forgetting the dangers of his situation, and was now trying to free as gently as possible the victim caught in the monstrous spider's web. When he had finished, he released the little bird. It joyfully fluttered its wings and flew away.

Nicholl was compassionately watching it vanish in the foliage when he heard these words spoken with feeling:

"You're a brave man! And a kind man!"

He turned around.

"Michel Ardan! What are you doing here?"

"I've come to shake your hand, Captain Nicholl, and prevent you from either killing Barbicane or being killed by him."

"Barbicane!" exclaimed the captain. "I've been looking for him for two hours and I can't find him! Where is he hiding?"

"That's not polite!" said Ardan. "One must always respect one's adversary. Don't worry: if Barbicane is alive, we'll find him, especially since, if he hasn't stopped to rescue a bird in distress the way you did, he must be looking for you too. But when we do find him, I assure you there won't be any question of a duel between you."

"Between Barbicane and me," Nicholl replied gravely, "there's a rivalry so great that only the death of one of us..."

"Come, come! Good men like you two may hate each other, but you also respect each other. You won't fight."

"I will."

"No."

"Captain," J. T. Maston said with heartfelt emotion, "I'm Barbicane's closest friend, his alter ego. If you really had to kill someone, shoot me: it will be exactly the same thing."

"Sir," said Nicholl, convulsively gripping his rifle, "such jokes..."

"Mr. Maston isn't joking," said Ardan, "and I understand his idea of dying for the man he's devoted to! But you're not going to shoot anyone, because I have such an attractive proposal to make to you and Barbicane that you'll both be eager to accept it."

"What is it?" Nicholl asked with obvious incredulity.

"Be patient. I can't tell you what it is unless Barbicane is present too."

"Then let's find him," said the captain.

The three men set off at once. After uncocking his rifle, Nicholl rested it on his shoulder and walked along with an abrupt stride, without saying a word.

For another half hour, the search was fruitless. J. T. Maston had an ominous foreboding. He watched Nicholl sternly, wondering whether he might not already have satisfied his vengeance and whether Barbicane might not be lying lifeless in some bloody thicket with a bullet in his heart. Ardan seemed to have the same thought. They were both casting suspicious glances at Nicholl when J. T. Maston suddenly stopped.

Twenty paces away they saw the motionless bust of a man sitting with his back against a gigantic catalpa tree half hidden in the grass.

"There he is!" said J. T. Maston.

Barbicane still did not move. Ardan looked intently into Nicholl's eyes, but saw no sign of guilt. He stepped forward and shouted:

"Barbicane! Barbicane!"

No answer. Ardan rushed up to his friend, but just as he was about to clasp him in his arms he stopped short and uttered an exclamation of surprise.

Barbicane, pencil in hand, was writing formulas and sketching geometrical figures in a notebook. His uncocked rifle lay on the ground.

Engrossed in his work, he too had forgotten his duel and his vengeance, and he had neither seen nor heard anything.

But when Michel Ardan put his hand on his arm he stood up and stared at him in surprise.

"Ah, it's you!" he said at length. "I've found it, my friend, I've found it!"

"You've found what?"

"The means!"

"What means?"

"The means of softening the blow inside the projectile when it's fired!"

"Really?" said Ardan, looking at Nicholl out of the corner of his eye.

"Yes! It's simply water, water that will act as a spring... Ah, Maston! You too!"

"Yes, it's Maston," said Ardan, "and allow me to introduce Captain Nicholl!"

"Nicholl!" cried Barbicane, leaping to his feet. "Excuse me, Captain, I'd forgotten... I'm ready..."

Ardan intervened before the two enemies had time to challenge each other again.

"It's a good thing the two of you didn't meet sooner this morning!" he said. "We'd now be mourning for one or both of you. But, thanks to God, who took a hand in the matter, there's no longer anything to fear. When a man forgets his hatred to plunge into problems of mechanics or rob a spider of his breakfast, it means that his hatred isn't dangerous for anyone."

And he told Barbicane how he had come upon Nicholl in the woods.

"And now tell me," he said in conclusion, "whether you think two fine men like you were made to shoot holes in each other!"

There was something so unexpected in the somewhat ridiculous situation that Barbicane and Nicholl were uncertain as to what attitude they ought to adopt toward each other. Ardan sensed this, and he decided to hasten their reconciliation.

"My good friends," he said with his best smile, "there's never been anything between you but a misunderstanding. Nothing more. To prove that it's all over, and since you've already proved that you're not afraid to risk your lives, accept the proposal I'm about to make to you."

"Tell us what it is," said Nicholl.

"Our friend Barbicane believes his projectile will go straight to the moon."

"I certainly do," said Barbicane.

"And our friend Nicholl is convinced that it will fall back to earth."

"I'm sure of it," said the captain.

"I don't claim to be able to make you agree with each other," said Ardan, "but I will say this to you: Leave inside the projectile with me, and we'll see whether we reach our destination or not."

"What!" exclaimed J. T. Maston, stupefied.

On hearing this sudden suggestion, the two rivals observed each other carefully. Barbicane waited for Nicholl's answer. Nicholl waited for Barbicane to speak.

"Well?" Ardan said in his most charming tone. "Why not, since the problem of the initial jolt has been solved?"

"I'll do it!" said Barbicane.

But before he had finished saying these words, Nicholl had said them too.

"Hurrah! Bravo! Vivat!" cried Michel Ardan, holding out his hands to the two rivals. "And now that the matter has been settled, my friends, allow me to treat you in the French manner. Let's go to breakfast."

CHAPTER 22

A NEW CITIZEN OF THE UNITED STATES

THAT DAY, all America learned of the duel between Nicholl and Barbicane and its singular outcome. The part played in it by the chivalrous Frenchman, his unexpected proposal which resolved the difficulty, the simultaneous acceptance by the two rivals, the way France and America were going to be united in the conquest of the moon—everything combined to make Michel Ardan's popularity still greater. The frenzied devotion that the Americans can show for an individual is well known. It is easy to imagine the passion stirred up by the daring Frenchman in a country where solemn magistrates harness themselves to a dancer's carriage and pull it in a triumphal procession. If Ardan's horses were not unharnessed, it is probably because he had none, but all other demonstrations of enthusiasm were showered on him. There was not one citizen who did not unite with him in heart and mind. *E pluribus unum,* as the motto of the United States puts it.

From that day on, Michel Ardan never had a moment of rest. He was constantly harassed by delegations from all parts of the country. The hands he shook and the people he smiled at were beyond all counting. He was soon exhausted; his voice, made hoarse by innumerable speeches, escaped from his lips only in unintelligible sounds, and he nearly got gastroenteritis from the toasts he had to drink to every county in the Union. This success would have intoxicated anyone else from the beginning, but Ardan was able to maintain himself in a state of witty and charming semi-inebriation.

Among the groups of all kinds which assailed him, the "lunatics" were particularly aware of what they owed to the future conqueror of the moon. One day several of these poor people, rather numerous in America, came to him and asked to be allowed to return to their native land with him. Some of them claimed to be able to speak the lunar language and offered to teach it to him. He good-naturedly indulged their innocent mania and agreed to deliver messages to their friends on the moon.

"A strange madness!" he said to Barbicane after he had sent them away. "It's a madness that often strikes superior minds. One of our most famous scientists, Arago, told me that many sane and sober people became greatly excited and developed incredible peculiarities whenever the moon took possession of them. You don't believe in the influence of the moon on illnesses?"

"Hardly," said Barbicane.

"I don't believe in it either, yet history has recorded some facts that are at least surprising. During an epidemic in 1693, for example, the death rate went up on January 21, when there was an eclipse. The famous Bacon lost consciousness during eclipses of the moon and didn't regain it until they were completely over. King Charles VI had six fits of insanity in 1399, all of them during either the new moon or the full moon. Some doctors have classified epilepsy among illnesses that follow the phases of the moon. Nervous illnesses have often appeared to be influenced by it. Mead tells of a child who went into convulsions whenever the moon was in opposi-

tion. Gall noticed that the overexcitement of sickly people increased twice a month, at the time of the new moon
and the full moon. And there are countless observations
of the same kind on dizzy spells, malignant fevers, and
somnambulism, all tending to prove that the moon has a
mysterious influence on earthly illnesses."

"But how? Why?" asked Barbicane.

"Why? Well, I'll give you the same answer that Arago
repeated nineteen centuries after Plutarch: 'Perhaps it's
because it's not true!' "

In the midst of his triumph, Michel Ardan could not escape from any of the ordeals inherent in the position of a
famous man. Successful promoters wanted to exhibit
him. Barnum offered him a million dollars to allow him
to take him from town to town all over the United States
and show him off as though he were some kind of strange
animal. Ardan called him a mahout and sent him packing.

Although he refused to satisfy the public's curiosity,
his portraits, at least, circulated all over the world and occupied the place of honor in many an album. They were
printed in all formats: some were life-size, others were no
bigger than a postage stamp. Everyone was able to have
his hero in every pose imaginable: face, bust or full-
length, from the front, from the side, three-quarters or
from the back. Over a million and a half of them were
printed. Ardan had a fine chance to sell little parts of himself as relics, but he did not take advantage of it. If he had
wanted to sell his hairs for a dollar apiece, he still had
enough of them left to make his fortune!

The truth was that this popularity did not displease
him. Quite the contrary. He placed himself at the public's
disposal and corresponded with people all over the world.
His witty remarks were repeated and spread, especially those he had never made; many were lent to him, in

accordance with the French saying that one lends only to the rich.

There were women among his admirers as well as men. How many "good matches" he could have made, if he had taken it into his head to "settle down"! Old maids especially, those who had been withering on the vine for forty years, dreamed night and day in front of his photographs.

He could easily have found hundreds of wives, even if he had demanded that they go to the moon with him. Women are either fearless or afraid of everything. But since he had no intention of founding a Franco-American family on the moon, he refused.

"I'm not going up there to play the part of Adam with a daughter of Eve!" he said. "All I'd have to do would be to come across a snake, and then . . ."

As soon as he was finally able to get away from the too often repeated joys of triumph, he went with his friends to pay a visit to the cannon. He felt that he at least owed it a little attention. Besides, he had become an expert on ballistics since he had begun living with Barbicane, J. T. Maston, and their colleagues. His greatest pleasure was to tell those staunch artillerymen that they were nothing but charming and skillful murderers. He constantly made jokes on the subject. When he visited the cannon he admired it greatly and went down to the bottom of the gigantic tube that would soon send him on his way to the moon.

"At least this cannon won't hurt anyone," he said, "and that's a rather amazing quality in a cannon. But as for your weapons that destroy, burn, shatter, and kill, I don't even want to hear about them."

At this point we must report an incident involving J. T. Maston. When he heard Barbicane and Nicholl accept

Ardan's suggestion, he resolved to join them and make the group a foursome. One day he asked to be included in the journey. Barbicane, heartbroken, told him that the projectile could not carry so many passengers. In despair, J. T. Maston went to Ardan, who told him he must resign himself, and used *ad hominem* arguments.

"I hope you won't be offended by what I'm about to say, Maston, but, just between you and me, you're too incomplete to put in an appearance on the moon."

"Incomplete!" cried the valiant artilleryman.

"Yes, my good friend. Think what would happen if we met inhabitants up there. Would you like to give them a deplorable idea of what happens here on earth by telling them what war is, and showing them that we spend most of our time devouring each other and breaking each other's arms and legs, on a globe that could feed a hundred billion people and now has only a billion and a quarter? Come, come: you'd make them refuse to speak to us!"

"But if you're smashed to pieces when you land," said J. T. Maston, "you'll be as incomplete as I am!"

"That's true, but we won't be smashed to pieces," replied Ardan.

His confidence was based partly on the fact that on October 18 a preparatory experiment had given excellent results. Wishing to study the initial jolt inside a projectile, Barbicane had sent for a thirty-two-inch mortar from the naval base at Pensacola. It was set up on the shore of the bay, so that its shells would fall into the sea. A hollow shell was carefully prepared for the singular experiment. The inside walls were lined with thick padding over springs made of the finest steel, forming a kind of nest.

"What a shame I can't get into it!" said J. T. Maston,

regretting that his size prevented him from participating directly in the experiment.

In this charming shell, which could be closed by means of a cover that screwed into place, Barbicane placed first a big cat, then a squirrel that belonged to J. T. Maston and was his favorite pet. He wanted to know how this little animal, which was not likely to suffer from dizziness, would be affected by the experimental journey.

The mortar was loaded with 160 pounds of powder and the shell was put in place. The weapon was fired.

The projectile shot out of the barrel, majestically described its parabola, reached an altitude of about a thousand feet, and moved downward in a graceful curve until it plunged into the water.

A boat hurried to the spot where it had fallen. Skilled divers leapt into the water and attached cables to the ears of the shell, which was quickly hoisted aboard the boat. Less than five minutes had gone by from the time the animals were enclosed to the time when the cover of their prison was unscrewed.

Ardan, Barbicane, Maston, and Nicholl were in the boat, and they watched the operation with a feeling of interest that is easy to understand. As soon as the shell was opened, the cat jumped out, a little rumpled but full of life, and showing no signs of having just returned from an aerial expedition. But there was no squirrel. They looked carefully. Not a trace of him. They had to face the truth: the cat had eaten his traveling companion.

J. T. Maston was greatly saddened by the loss of his poor squirrel, though he was somewhat consoled by the knowledge that he was a martyr to science.

After this experiment, all hesitation and fear vanished. Furthermore, Barbicane's plans were to improve the projectile still more and almost entirely eliminate the effects of the initial jolt. There was nothing left to do but leave.

Two days later, Michel Ardan received a message from the President of the United States. He fully appreciated the honor. Like his chivalrous compatriot, the Marquis de La Fayette, he had been made an honorary citizen of the United States of America.

CHAPTER 23

THE PROJECTILE COACH

AFTER THE completion of the famous cannon, public interest turned to the projectile, the new vehicle that would take the three bold adventurers into space. No one had forgotten that in his cablegram of September 30 Michel Ardan had asked for a modification of the plans drawn up by the members of the committee.

Barbicane had rightly thought that the shape of the projectile was unimportant, for, after going through the earth's atmosphere in a few seconds, it would be moving in an absolute vacuum. The committee had agreed on a spherical shape so that the projectile could spin and behave as it pleased. But now that it was going to be transformed into a vehicle, it was another matter. Michel Ardan did not want to travel like a squirrel in a cage; he wanted to have his head up and his feet down, with as much dignity as if he were in the basket of a balloon, though he would, of course, be moving much more swiftly. He had no desire to turn unseemly somersaults during his journey.

New plans were sent to Breadwill & Co. in Albany, with instructions to begin work without delay. The redesigned projectile was cast on November 2 and immediately sent to Stone Hill by means of the eastern railroads. It arrived undamaged on November 10. Ardan, Barbicane, and Nicholl were impatiently awaiting the "projectile coach" in which they were going to set off to discover a new world.

No one can deny that it was a magnificent piece of work, a metallurgical product that was a great credit to American industrial genius. It was the first time that aluminum had ever been obtained in such a large mass, and this alone was rightly regarded as a prodigious feat. The precious projectile sparkled in the sunlight. With its impressive size and its conical cap it might have been taken for one of those thick pepper-box turrets which medieval architects placed at the corners of fortresses. It lacked only loopholes and a weathervane.

"I expect," said Michel Ardan, "to see soldiers come out of it carrying arquebuses and wearing chain mail. We'll be like feudal lords up there, and with a little artillery we'll be able to hold off all the armies on the moon, if there are any."

"So you like the vehicle?" asked Barbicane.

"Yes, of course," replied Ardan, who had been examining it from an artistic point of view. "I only regret that it doesn't have a more slender shape and a more graceful cone. It might have had a cluster of metal ornaments on the end, with a chimera, for example, or a gargoyle, or a phoenix coming out of the fire with outspread wings and open mouth..."

"What for?" asked Barbicane, whose practical mind was not very sensitive to the beauties of art.

"What for? Since you ask me the reason, I'm afraid you'll never understand it!"

"Tell me anyway, my friend."

"Well, I feel that we should always put a little art into what we do. It's better that way. Do you know an Indian play called *The Child's Cart*?"

"Never heard of it."

"I'm not surprised," said Ardan. "In that play there's a thief who's about to cut a hole in the wall of a house but can't decide whether to give his hole the shape of a lyre, a flower, a bird, or an amphora. Now tell me, Barbicane, if you had been a member of the jury, would you have condemned that thief?"

"Without hesitation," replied Barbicane, "especially since he was also guilty of housebreaking."

"And I would have acquitted him! That's why you'll never be able to understand me!"

"I won't even try, my valiant artist."

"Since the outside of our projectile coach leaves something to be desired, I hope I'll at least be allowed to furnish it with all the luxury befitting ambassadors from the earth."

"As far as the inside is concerned, you can arrange it any way you like!"

But before going on to the esthetic Barbicane had concerned himself with the practical, and the system he had invented for lessening the effects of the initial jolt was constructed with perfect precision.

He had told himself, not without reason, that no spring would be strong enough to deaden the impact, and during his famous stroll in the Skersnaw Woods he had finally resolved this great difficulty in an ingenious way. He was going to call on water to render him that outstanding service. Here is how.

The projectile was to be filled with water to a height of three feet. Over it would be a waterproof wooden disk fitting tightly against the inner wall but able to slide on it. The three passengers would be on this circular raft. The water would be divided by horizontal partitions which the first shock would break successively. Each layer of water would be driven upward through pipes, and would thus act as a spring, while the disk, equipped with strong buffers, would not be able to strike the bottom until each of the partitions had been broken. The passengers would no doubt still experience a violent impact after all the water had been driven out, but Barbicane expected the first shock to be entirely deadened by this extremely strong spring.

It is true that three feet of water with a surface area of fifty-four square feet would weigh nearly 11,500 pounds, but, according to Barbicane, the propulsive force of the cannon would be enough to overcome this increase in weight; furthermore, the water would all be driven out in less than a second, and the projectile would then resume its normal weight.

Such was Barbicane's solution to the serious problem of the initial shock. The work was intelligently understood and capably executed by the engineers of Breadwill & Co. Once the effect had been produced and the water had been driven out the passengers could easily get rid of the broken partitions and take apart the sliding disk that would support them at the moment of departure.

As for the upper walls of the projectile, they were covered with thick leather padding over coils of fine steel which had the flexibility of watch springs. The pipes through which the water would escape were completely hidden beneath this padding.

Thus every imaginable precaution had been taken to deaden the initial shock. "If we let ourselves be crushed now," said Michel Ardan, "we'll have to be made of very bad material."

The projectile had an outside diameter of nine feet and a height of twelve feet. In order not to exceed the assigned weight, the thickness of its walls had been reduced a little, and its bottom, which would have to withstand the violent thrust of the gases produced by the explosion of the guncotton, was reinforced. This is how bombs and cylindroconical shells are made: their bottoms are always thicker than their sides.

Entrance into this metal tower was by way of a narrow opening in the cone which looked like the manhole in a steam boiler. It was hermetically closed by means of an aluminum plate firmly bolted in place from the inside. The passengers would thus be able to leave their mobile prison when they reached the moon.

But it was not enough for them to go: they must also be able to see on the way. This was easily arranged. Under the padding were four portholes with panes of thick optical glass; two were in the circular wall of the projectile, one was in its bottom, and another was in its conical cap, so that the passengers would be able to see the receding earth, the approaching moon, and the starry reaches of space. These portholes were protected against the initial shock by solidly embedded steel plates which could be opened from the inside by bolts. In this way, the air in the projectile could not escape, and observation was possible.

All these admirably constructed mechanisms functioned perfectly, and the engineers had shown equal intelligence in the inner fittings of the projectile.

There were solidly attached containers for food and water. The passengers could even have fire and light by means of gas stored in a special container at a pressure of several atmospheres. They would only have to turn on a faucet. There was enough gas to heat and light the comfortable vehicle for six days. It can be seen that nothing was lacking in the way of necessities for life and even well-being. And, thanks to Michel Ardan's artistic instincts, the pleasant was joined to the useful in the form of art objects. He would have made his projectile into a veritable artist's studio if he had not been short of space.

It would be a mistake to assume that three people had to be cramped in that metal tower. It had an area of fifty-four square feet and a height of about ten feet, enough to give the passengers a certain freedom of movement. They would not have been more at ease in the most comfortable railroad car in the United States.

When the question of food and light had been settled, there still remained the question of air. It was obvious that the air in the projectile would not be enough for four days. In an hour, one man consumes all the oxygen in about twenty-five gallons of air. Barbicane, his two companions, and the two dogs they intended to bring with them would consume six hundred gallons of oxygen, or about seven pounds, in twenty-four hours. The air in the projectile would therefore have to be renewed. How? By a very simple process, that of Reiset and Regnault, that Michael Ardan had referred to during the discussion at the meeting.

Air is composed, practically speaking, of twenty-one percent oxygen and seventy-nine percent nitrogen. What happens when we breathe? It is a simple phenomenon. We absorb oxygen, which is necessary for sustaining life, from the air, and expel the nitrogen intact. Exhaled air has lost nearly five percent of its oxygen and contains an almost equal volume of carbonic acid, the end product of the combustion of the elements of the blood by the inhaled oxygen. In a closed space, therefore, after a certain time all the oxygen in the air will be replaced by carbonic acid, which is an essentially noxious gas.

The question came down to this: with the nitrogen conserved intact, how could the oxygen be replenished and how could the carbonic acid be destroyed? It was quite easy, by means of potassium chlorate and caustic potash.

Potassium chlorate is a salt which exists in the form of white flakes. When it is heated to a temperature above four hundred degrees centigrade, it is transformed into potassium chloride, and the oxygen it contains is entirely given off. Eighteen pounds of potassium chlorate yields seven pounds of oxygen: the amount the passengers needed for twenty-four hours. So much for replenishing the oxygen.

As for caustic potash, it has a strong affinity for the carbonic acid mingled in the air. It need only be agitated in order to make it combine with the carbonic acid and form potassium bicarbonate. So much for absorbing the carbonic acid.

By combining these two processes, it was possible to restore all the life-giving properties to the exhaled air. The two chemists, Reiset and Regnault, had shown this experimentally. But it must be said that so far the experiment had been performed only with animals. However great its scientific precision, its effect on men was still completely unknown.

These were the facts that Michel Ardan pointed out during the meeting at which the important question was considered. Not wishing to leave any doubt about the possibility of living on that artificial air, he offered to try it himself before the departure. But the honor of making the test was energetically demanded by J. T. Maston.

"Since I'm not going with you," he said, "the least you can do is to let me live in the projectile for a week or so."

The others would have been unkind to refuse him. They granted his request. He was given enough food, water, potassium chlorate, and caustic potash for eight days; then on November 12, at six o'clock in the morning, after having shaken hands with his friends and expressly instructed them not to open his prison until six o'clock on the evening of November 20, he slipped into the projectile and the opening was hermetically sealed behind him.

What happened inside the projectile during the eight days? It was impossible to tell. The thickness of its walls prevented all sounds from reaching the outside.

On November 20, at exactly six o'clock, the cover was removed from the opening. J. T. Maston's friends were a little worried, but they were promptly reassured when they heard a loud, joyful "Hurrah!"

J. T. Maston soon appeared at the top of the cone in a triumphant pose. He had gained weight!

CHAPTER 24

THE LONGS PEAK TELESCOPE

O N OCTOBER 20 of the previous year, after the closing of the subscription, Barbicane had turned over to the Cambridge Observatory the money necessary for the construction of an enormous telescope. This telescope, whether a refracting or a reflecting one, was to be powerful enough to detect an object no more than nine feet wide on the surface of the moon.

There is an important difference between a refracting and a reflecting telescope; it will be best to recall it here. A refracting telescope is composed of a tube which has at its upper end a convex lens called the objective, and at its lower end a second lens known as the ocular, to which the observer applies his eye. Light rays from the object pass through the first lens and, by refraction, form an inverted image at its focus.* This image is observed through the ocular, which enlarges it exactly like a magnifying glass. Thus the tube of a refracting telescope is closed at both ends by the objective and the ocular.

The reflecting telescope, on the other hand, is open at its upper end. Light rays from the observed object penetrate it freely and strike a concave, i.e., converging, metal mirror. From there they are reflected to a small mirror

---

*The point at which the light rays are reunited after having been refracted.

that sends them to the ocular, which is so disposed as to magnify the image produced.

Thus in a refracting telescope it is refraction that plays the principal role, while in a reflecting telescope it is reflection. The former is sometimes called simply a refractor, the latter a reflector. The difficulty in making them lies almost entirely in making the objective, whether it be a lens or a metal mirror.

At the time when the Gun Club was preparing for its great experiment, these instruments had been highly perfected and gave magnificent results. Science had come a long way since the days when Galileo observed the heavenly bodies with his poor little seven-power refracting telescope. Since the sixteenth century, telescopes had grown considerably wider and longer, and had made it possible to probe more deeply into interstellar space. Among the refracting telescopes in operation at that time were the one at the Pulkovo Observatory in Russia, with a fifteen-inch objective;* the one made by the French optician Lerebours, also with a fifteen-inch objective; and the one at the Cambridge Observatory, with a nineteen-inch objective.

Among the reflecting telescopes there were some of remarkable power and gigantic size. The first one, made by Herschel, had a length of thirty-six feet, a mirror with a diameter of four and a half feet, and a magnification of six thousand. The second one was in Birr, Ireland, and belonged to Lord Rosse. It was forty-eight feet long, its mirror was six feet in diameter,** and its magnification was 6,400; an im-

---

*It cost 80,000 rubles ($60,000).

**One often hears of refracting telescopes of much greater length. One of them, with a length of 300 feet, was installed, under Domini Cassini's direction, at the Paris Observatory. But it should be pointed out that these telescopes had no tube. The objective was suspended in the air by means of masts, and the observer, holding his ocular in his hand, placed himself as close to the focus of the objective as possible. It is easy to understand how difficult these instruments were to use, and particularly how difficult it was to center two lenses under such conditions.

mense stone structure had to be built to house the instruments for maneuvering it, and to support its weight of 28,000 pounds.

Despite these colossal dimensions, however, the magnification obtained never went very far beyond six thousand. A magnification of six thousand brings the moon to an apparent distance of thirty-nine miles and makes it possible to see objects with a width of no less than sixty feet, unless they are extremely long.

In order to see the Gun Club's projectile, which was nine feet wide and fifteen feet long, the moon would have to be brought to an apparent distance of five miles or less, and this would require a magnification of 48,000.

Such was the problem faced by the Cambridge Observatory. It would not be stopped by financial difficulties, but there were still physical difficulties to be overcome.

First of all, a choice had to be made between a refractor and a reflector. Refractors have certain advantages over reflectors. With the same objective diameter they make it possible to obtain greater magnification, because light rays passing through the lenses lose less by absorption than by reflection from the metal mirror of a reflector. But the thickness that can be given to a lens is limited: if the lens is too thick, it will not let light rays pass through it. Furthermore, the construction of such enormous lenses is difficult and the time is measured in years.

Therefore, even though the images are illuminated better in a refractor—an appreciable advantage in observing the moon, whose light is simply reflected—it was decided to use a reflector, which can be made more quickly and permits greater magnification. And since light rays lose a great deal of their intensity in passing through the earth's atmosphere, the Gun Club decided to put the telescope on one of the highest mountains in the country, which would diminish the amount of air that would have to be traversed by the light.

As we have seen, in a reflecting telescope the ocular—that is, the magnifying glass placed before the observer's eye—produces the magnification, and the greater the diameter and focal distance of the objective, the greater the magnification it will allow. To obtain a magnification of 48,000, the size of Herschel's and Lord Rosse's objectives would have to be far surpassed. There lay the difficulty, for the casting of such mirrors is a very delicate operation.

Fortunately a few years earlier a scientist at the Institut de France, Léon Foucault, had invented a way of greatly reducing the time required for polishing an objective by replacing metal mirrors with silvered glass ones. One had only to cast a piece of glass to the right size, then plate it with silver. This process, which gives excellent results, was used in making the objective.

It was arranged in accordance with Herschel's method. In his big telescope, the image of the object, reflected by the inclined mirror at one end of the tube, was formed at its other end, where the ocular was situated. Thus the observer, instead of being placed at the lower end of the tube, raised himself to its upper end, and there, with his magnifying glass, he looked into the enormous cylinder. This system had the advantage of eliminating the little mirror whose function was to reflect the image to the ocular, so the image was reflected only once instead of twice. Therefore fewer light rays were absorbed, the image was less weakened, and greater brightness was obtained.* This would be a valuable advantage in observing the projectile.

When these decisions had been made, the work was begun. According to the Cambridge Observatory's calculations, the new telescope would have to be 280 feet long, and its mirror would have to have a diameter of sixteen feet. However colossal it might be, it would not be comparable to the 10,000-foot telescope that the astronomer Hooke proposed building several years ago. Nevertheless its construction presented great difficulties.

As for the question of location, it was quickly settled. A high mountain had to be chosen, and high mountains are not numerous in the United States.

The mountains of that great country are composed of two ranges of medium height. Between them flows the magnificent Mississippi, which the Americans would call "the king of rivers" if they were willing to accept any kind of royalty.

In the east are the Appalachians, whose tallest peak, in New Hampshire, is 6,600 feet high, which is quite modest.

In the west are the Rocky Mountains, an immense range which begins at the Straits of Magellan, runs along the west coast of South America under the name of the Andes, crosses the Isthmus of Panama, and extends across North America all the way to the Arctic.

These mountains are not very high; the Alps or the Himalayas would look down on them from their lofty heights. Their tallest peak is only 11,771 feet high, whereas Mont Blanc is 15,787 feet high, and Kinchinjunga, the

*These reflectors are called "front view telescopes."

highest of the Himalayas, rises 29,454 feet above sea level.

But since the members of the Gun Club wanted the telescope as well as the cannon to be within the boundaries of the United States, they had to content themselves with the Rocky Mountains. All the necessary materials and equipment were sent to Longs Peak, in Colorado Territory.

The difficulties of all kinds that the American engineers had to overcome, and the wonders of daring and skill that they accomplished, could not be described by tongue or pen. It was a truly spectacular feat. Huge stones, heavy forged parts, enormous pieces of the cylinder, and the objective, with a weight of 30,000 pounds, had to be brought up above the snow line, over 10,000 feet high, after having been brought across deserted prairies and through dense forests and fearful rapids, far from all centers of population, in wild regions where each detail of life became an almost insoluble problem. But the Americans' genius triumphed over these countless obstacles. In late September, less than a year after work had begun, the gigantic tube of the telescope, 284 feet long, was pointing into the air. It was suspended from an enormous iron framework; an ingenious mechanism enabled the observer to aim it at any point in the sky and follow the heavenly bodies from one horizon to the other as they moved through space.

It has cost more than $400,000. The first time it was aimed at the moon, the observers were both curious and apprehensive. What were they going to discover in the field of that 48,000-power telescope? Populations, herds of lunar animals, cities, lakes, oceans? No, they saw nothing that science had not known already. They were, however, able to determine the moon's volcanic nature with absolute precision.

Before serving the Gun Club, the Longs Peak telescope rendered immense services to astronomy. With its great power, it was able to scan the outermost reaches of the heavens; the apparent diameters of stars were rigorously measured, and Mr. Clarke of the Cambridge Observatory decomposed the crab nebula in Taurus, which Lord Rosse's telescope had never been able to resolve.

CHAPTER 25

FINAL DETAILS

IT WAS November 22. The supreme departure was to take place ten days later. Only one operation remained to be carried out, a dangerous, delicate operation that required infinite precautions, and against whose success Captain Nicholl had made his third bet: the operation of loading the cannon, of putting the 400,000 pounds of guncotton into it. Nicholl had thought, not without reason, perhaps, that the handling of such a formidable quantity of guncotton would bring on a grave catastrophe, or at any rate that the eminently explosive mass would ignite itself under the pressure of the projectile.

The serious dangers involved were increased still more by the carelessness and unconcern of the Americans, who, during the Civil War, did not hesitate to load their bombshells with cigars in their mouths. But Barbicane was determined that his experiment would not fail before it even got under way; he chose his best workers, kept his eye on them at all times and, by caution and precautions, was able to put the chances of success in his favor.

First of all, he was careful not to bring the whole charge into the enclosure at once. He had it brought in little by little in tightly sealed caissons. The 400,000 pounds of guncotton was divided into 500-pound portions and placed in 800 cartridge bags made by the best craftsmen in Pensacola. The caissons held ten bags each. They came in one by one on the railroad from Tampa. In that way there was never any more than 5,000 pounds of guncotton within the enclosure at any given time. As soon as each caisson arrived it was unloaded by barefoot workers. The cartridge bags were taken to the cannon and lowered into it by means of hand cranes. All steam machinery had been removed from the vicinity, and all fires had been put out for two miles around. Merely protecting that mass of guncotton from the heat of the sun, even in November, was a major concern. The work was done preferably at night, with the aid of a Ruhmkorff apparatus which cast bright light all the way to the bottom of the cannon. There the cartridge bags were stacked with perfect regularity and connected with the wires that were to bring an electric spark to the center of each one of them simultaneously, for it was by means of a battery that the guncotton was going to be ignited.

The wires, surrounded by an insulating material, were united into a single cable that passed through an opening in the wall of the cannon just below the height at which the projectile was to be placed, then went up to the surface of the ground through a hole in the stonework that had been made for that purpose. When it reached the top of Stone Hill, the cable continued for a distance of two miles, supported by poles, until it reached a powerful Bunsen battery, after passing through a switch. One would have only to push the button of the switch to make the current flow and ignite the 400,000 pounds of guncotton. Needless to say, the battery was not to be activated until the last moment.

By November 28 the 800 cartridge bags were stacked at the bottom of the cannon. This part of the operation had been successful. But what worries, apprehensions, and struggles Barbicane had been through! He had vainly tried to keep all visitors away from Stone Hill: every day people had climbed over the stockade, and some of them had carried lack of caution to the point of madness by smoking in the midst of the bags of guncotton. Barbicane had flown into a rage several times a day. J. T. Maston had helped as best he could, driving away intruders with great vigor and picking up the burning cigar butts they had tossed here and there. It was a hard job, because there were more than 300,000 people thronged around the enclosure. Michel Ardan had volunteered to escort the caissons to the mouth of the cannon, but when Barbicane saw him holding a big cigar between his lips as he chased away careless bystanders and gave them a bad example at the same time, he realized that he could not count on that daring smoker, and he had to have him watched more closely than anyone else.

Finally, since there is a God for artillerymen, nothing blew up and the loading operation was completed. Captain Nicholl was in serious danger of losing the third part of his bet, although the projectile still had to be placed in the cannon and lowered onto the deep pile of guncotton.

But before beginning that operation, the objects necessary for the journey were methodically stowed in the projectile. There were quite a few of them, and if Michel Ardan had been allowed to have his way they would soon have taken up all the space reserved for the passengers. The charming Frenchman had an incredible number of things that he wanted to take to the moon, and they were as useless as they were numerous. But Barbicane intervened and the list of objects was reduced to what was strictly necessary.

Several thermometers, barometers, and telescopes were placed in the instrument chest.

The passengers were curious to examine the moon during the journey; to facilitate their scrutiny of that new world they decided to take Beer and Moedler's excellent map, the *Mappa Selenographica,* printed in four sheets and rightly regarded as a masterpiece of observation and patience. It reproduced with scrupulous accuracy the slightest details of that portion of the moon which is turned toward the earth; mountains, valleys, basins, craters, peaks, and rills were shown with their exact dimensions, correct locations and names, from Mount Doerfel and Mount Leibnitz, whose tall peak stands in the eastern part of the visible disk, to the Mare Frigoris, which lies in the northern circumpolar region. It was a valuable document for the three explorers, because they could already study the new land before they had ever set foot on it.

They also took three shotguns and three repeating rifles that fired explosive bullets, plus a large quantity of ammunition.

"We don't know whom we may run into," said Michel Ardan. "There may be men or animals that won't appreciate our coming to pay them a visit. We must take precautions."

These defensive weapons were accompanied by picks, mattocks, saws, and other indispensable tools, and clothes suited to all temperatures, from the cold of the polar regions to the heat of the torrid zone.

Michel Ardan would have liked to take along a certain number of animals, though not a couple of each species, for he saw no need to stock the moon with snakes, tigers, alligators, and other harmful beasts.

"No," he said to Barbicane, "but a few beasts of burden, such as oxen, cows, donkeys or horses, would look good in the landscape and be very useful to us."

"I agree," replied Barbicane, "but our projectile isn't Noah's ark; it has neither the same capacity nor the same destination. Let's stay within the limits of the possible."

Finally, after long discussions, it was agreed that they would content themselves with taking along an excellent hunting bitch belonging to Captain Nicholl and a vigorous, prodigiously strong Newfoundland dog. Several boxes of useful seeds were numbered among the essential objects. If Michel Ardan had had his way, he would also have taken a few bags of soil to plant them in. He did, however, take a dozen shrubs that were carefully wrapped in a straw covering and stowed in the projectile.

There was still the important matter of food, for they had to take into account the possibility that they would land on a barren portion of the moon. Barbicane arranged to take a year's supply. This is not surprising when one considers that the food consisted of canned meat and vegetables reduced to their minimum volume by a hydraulic press, and that they contained a large amount of nutritive elements. They had little variety, but one could not be particular on such an expedition. There was also fifty gallons of brandy, and enough water for only two months; as a result of the astronomers' latest observations, no one had any doubt that there was a certain amount of water on the moon. As for food, it would have been foolish to believe that inhabitants of the earth would not find anything to eat up there. Michel Ardan did not have the slightest doubt on the subject. If he had, he would have decided not to go.

"Besides," he said one day to his friends, "we won't be completely abandoned by our comrades on earth, and they won't forget us."

"Certainly not," said J. T. Maston.

"What do you mean?" asked Nicholl.

"It's quite simple," replied Ardan. "The cannon will still be here, won't it? Well, each time the moon is in a favorable position as far as zenith or perigee is concerned, which will be about once a year, can't our friends send us a projectile full of food, which we'll be expecting on a certain day?"

"Of course!" cried J. T. Maston in the tone of a man who has just conceived an idea. "That's an excellent plan! We won't forget you!"

"I'm sure you won't. So we'll have regular news from the earth, and we'll be terribly inept if we don't find some way of communicating with our friends down here!"

These words were spoken with such confidence that Michel Ardan, with his air of determination and his superb self-assurance, could have persuaded the whole Gun Club to come with him. What he said seemed simple, elementary, easy, and sure to succeed, and a man would have had to have a truly sordid attachment to this terrestrial globe not to accompany the three explorers on their lunar expedition.

When the various objects had been stowed in the projectile, the water that would act as a spring was poured between the partitions and the gas was compressed into its container. As for the potassium chlorate and the caustic potash, Barbicane, fearing unexpected delays on the way, took enough to replenish the oxygen and absorb the carbonic acid for two months. An ingenious automatic apparatus was installed to purify the air and restore its life-giving properties. The projectile was now ready, and all that remained to be done was to lower it into the cannon. This was going to be an operation filled with difficulties and perils.

The enormous shell was brought to the top of Stone Hill, where powerful cranes seized it and held it suspended above the deep metal pit.

This was the crucial moment. If the chains had broken from the immense weight, the fall of such a mass would surely have made the guncotton explode.

Fortunately this did not happen, and a few hours later the projectile, having been slowly lowered down the bore of the cannon, was resting on its explosive cushion of guncotton. Its weight had no other effect than to compress the charge more tightly.

"I've lost," said Captain Nicholl, handing Barbicane three thousand dollars.

Barbicane did not want to take the money from his traveling companion, but he had to yield to Nicholl's insistence; the captain wanted to fulfill all his obligations before leaving the earth.

"Then I have only one wish for you, my brave captain," said Michel Ardan.

"What is it?" asked Nicholl.

"That you'll lose your other two bets! If you do, we'll at least be sure of getting under way."

CHAPTER 26

FIRE!

THE FIRST day of December had arrived. It was a fateful day, for if the projectile was not fired that evening at forty-six minutes and forty seconds past ten o'clock, more than eighteen years would go by before the moon was in the same simultaneous conditions of zenith and perigee.

The weather was magnificent. Despite the approach of winter, the sun was shining brightly on the globe that was about to lose three of its inhabitants to another world.

How many people had slept badly during the night that had preceded this impatiently desired day! How many breasts were oppressed by the heavy burden of waiting! All hearts were palpitating with anxiety, except Michel Ardan's. Unperturbed, he came and went with his usual hurry and bustle, without showing any sign of unwonted concern. He had slept peacefully, like Turenne sleeping on a gun carriage before a battle.

Since dawn a vast crowd had covered the plain that stretched out around Stone Hill as far as the eye could see. Every quarter of an hour the railroad brought a new load of onlookers. This immigration soon took on fantastic proportions. According to the *Tampa Observer,* five million people trod the soil of Florida on that memorable day.

For a month the greater part of that crowd had been camping around the enclosure and laying the foundations of a town that has since come to be known as Ardanville. The plain was bristling with huts, shanties, and cabins, and these ephemeral dwellings housed a population large enough to arouse the envy of the biggest cities in Europe.

Every nation on earth was represented there; all the world's languages were spoken at once, as though the days of the Tower of Babel had returned. The various classes of American society were mingled in absolute equality. Bankers, farmers, sailors, buyers, brokers, cotton planters, merchants, boatmen, and magistrates rubbed elbows with primitive unceremoniousness. Louisiana Creoles fraternized with Indiana farmers; gentlemen from Kentucky or Tennessee and elegant, haughty Virginians conversed with half-savage trappers from the Great Lakes and cattle merchants from Cincinnati. Wearing broad-brimmed white beaver hats or classic Panamas, trousers made of blue cotton cloth from the factories at Poelousas, elegant unbleached linen jackets and brightly colored boots, they exhibited flamboyant batiste shirt fronts, and on their shirts, cuffs, ties, fingers, and ears glittered a wide assortment of rings, pins, diamonds, chains, earrings, and trinkets whose expensiveness was equaled only by their bad taste. Women, children, and servants, dressed with equal opulence, accompanied, followed, preceded, and surrounded those husbands, fathers, and masters who were like tribal chieftains in the midst of their abundant families.

At mealtimes it was an impressive sight when all those people began devouring, with an appetite that threatened the food supply of Florida, various dishes that were peculiar to the southern states and would have been rather repugnant to a European stomach, such as fricasseed frogs, braised monkey, fish chowder, roast opossum, and broiled raccoon.

And what a variety of liquors and other drinks came to the aid of that indigestible food! What exciting cries and inviting shouts rang out in barrooms and taverns adorned with glasses, mugs, flasks, decanters, incredibly shaped bottles, mortars for pounding sugar, and bundles of straws!

"Here's a mint julep!" cried a bartender.

"One Burgundy sangaree!"

"A gin sling!"

"A brandy smash!"

"Who wants to taste a real mint julep, made in the latest style?" a bartender called out enticingly, tossing the ingredients—sugar, lemon, mint, crushed ice, water, brandy, and fresh pineapple—from one glass to another with the deftness of a sleight-of-hand artist.

These invitations to throats made thirsty by hot spices were usually repeated loudly and simultaneously, producing a deafening uproar. But on this first day of December such shouts were rare. The bartenders could have yelled themselves hoarse without attracting any customers. No one was thinking of eating or drinking. At four o'clock there were many people in the crowd who had not yet eaten lunch. There was an even more significant symptom: the Americans' violent passion for games and gambling had been overcome by their excited anticipation. The sight of tenpins lying on their sides, dice sleeping in their cups, motionless roulette wheels, abandoned cribbage boards, and cards used for playing whist, blackjack, monte, and faro enclosed in their unopened boxes, showed clearly that the great event of the day overshadowed everything else and left no room for diversions.

Until evening an almost silent agitation, of the kind

that precedes great catastrophes, ran through that anxious crowd. Each mind was in the grip of an indescribable uneasiness, a painful torpor, an indefinable feeling that clutched the heart. Everyone wished it were already over.

At about seven o'clock, however, this heavy silence was suddenly dissipated. The moon rose above the horizon. Several million hurrahs greeted its appearance. It had come on time. Cheers rose up to the heavens and applause broke out on all sides while the blonde Phoebe shone placidly in a beautiful sky and caressed that feverish crowd with her most affectionate beams.

Just then the three dauntless explorers appeared. The cheering redoubled. Unanimously, instantaneously, the American national anthem burst from every heaving chest, and *Yankee Doodle,* sung in a chorus of five million, rose like a tempest of sound to the uppermost reaches of the atmosphere.

Then, after that irresistible surge of feeling, the anthem died away, the last voices gradually fell silent, the noises were dissipated and a quiet murmur floated above the deeply moved crowd. Meanwhile the Frenchman and the two Americans had entered the enclosure around which the crowd was gathered. They were accompanied by members of the Gun Club and delegations from European observatories. Barbicane, cool and calm, unhurriedly gave his final orders. Captain Nicholl, with his lips pressed tightly together and his hands behind his back, walked with firm, measured steps. Michel Ardan, still nonchalant, dressed like a typical traveler, with leather gaiters on his feet, a satchel slung over his shoulder, brown velvet clothes hanging loosely from his body, and a cigar held jauntily between his teeth, was distributing warm handshakes with princely prodigality as he walked along. His gaiety and high spirits were irrepress-

ible; he laughed, joked, and played childish tricks on the
dignified J. T. Maston; in short, he was French and, even
worse, Parisian to the end.

It was ten o'clock, time for the explorers to take their
places in the projectile. It would take a certain amount of
time to lower them to it, bolt the steel plate over the opening when they were inside, and remove the cranes and
scaffolding from the mouth of the cannon.

Murchison, who was going to ignite the guncotton by
means of an electric spark, had synchronized his chronometer to within a tenth of a second of Barbicane's. The
explorers in the projectile would thus be able to watch the
impassive moving hand that would mark the instant of
their departure.

The time for farewells had come. It was a touching
scene. Despite his feverish gaiety, Michel Ardan felt
moved. J. T. Maston had found under his dry lids an old
tear which he had no doubt reserved for this occasion. He
shed it on the forehead of his brave and beloved friend
Barbicane.

"Why don't I come with you?" he said. "There's still
time!"

"Impossible, my friend," replied Barbicane.

A few moments later, the three explorers had climbed
into the projectile and bolted it shut behind them. The
mouth of the cannon, entirely cleared, was open to the
sky.

Captain Nicholl, Barbicane, and Michel Ardan were
definitively enclosed in their metal vehicle.

Who could depict the universal excitement that now
reached its peak?

The moon was moving across a clear sky, extinguish-
ing the glittering stars on its path. It was now crossing the
constellation Gemini and was nearly halfway between the

horizon and the zenith. It was easy for everyone to understand that the projectile was going to be aimed ahead of its target, as a hunter aims in front of a running hare in order to hit it.

An awesome silence hung over the whole scene. There was not a breath of wind on the earth! Not a breath of air in any chest! Hearts no longer dared to beat. All fearful eyes were fixed on the gaping mouth of the cannon.

Murchison was watching the hand of his chronometer. Only forty more seconds, and each one of them was like a century.

At the twentieth second a quiver ran through the crowd and everyone realized that the daring explorers inside the projectile were also counting the terrible seconds. Isolated cries broke out:

"Thirty-five! . . . Thirty-six! . . . Thirty-seven! . . . Thirty eight! . . . Thirty-nine! . . . Forty! . . . *Fire!!!*"

Murchison pressed the switch and sent an electric spark into the depths of the cannon.

Instantly there was a terrifying, fantastic, superhuman detonation which could not be compared to thunder or any previously known sound, not even the eruption of a volcano. An immense spout of flame shot from the bowels of the earth as from a crater. The ground heaved, and only a few people caught a brief glimpse of the projectile victoriously cleaving the air amid clouds of glowing vapor.

CHAPTER 27

CLOUDY WEATHER

WHEN THE incandescent spout rose into the sky to a prodigious height, the blossoming flames lit up the whole Florida peninsula, and for an incalculable instant day was substituted for night over a considerable expanse of the country. The immense plume of fire was seen from a hundred miles at sea, in the Atlantic as well as in the Gulf of Mexico, and more than one ship's captain noted the appearance of that gigantic meteor in his log.

The firing of the cannon was accompanied by a veritable earthquake. Florida was shaken to its entrails. The gases released by the guncotton, expanded by heat, pushed back the layers of the atmosphere with incomparable violence, and this artificial hurricane, a hundred times swifter than any natural one, passed through the air like a monstrous whirlwind.

Not one spectator had remained standing: men, women, and children were all flattened like grain stalks before a storm. There was an indescribable tumult and many people were seriously injured. J. T. Maston, who, against all prudence, had stood too far forward, was thrown back fifty feet and his fellow citizens saw him pass overhead like a cannon ball. Three hundred thousand people were temporarily deafened and stupefied.

The violent wind blew down huts and cabins, uprooted

trees within a radius of twenty miles, drove trains all the way back to Tampa, struck the city like an avalanche, and destroyed over a hundred buildings, including Saint Mary's Church and the new stock exchange building, which was cracked from one end to the other. Several ships in the harbor were thrown against each other and sank. Others were tossed up on shore after having snapped their anchor chains as though they were threads.

But the area of destruction extended still further, beyond the borders of the United States. The effect of the concussion, aided by the west wind, was felt far out in the Atlantic, over three hundred miles from the American coast.

An artificial storm, which Admiral FitzRoy had been unable to foresee, struck his ships with incredible violence. Several vessels, including the *Childe Harold* of Liverpool, were caught in those frightful cyclones before they had time to lower their sails, and sank under full canvas, a regrettable disaster which became the subject of vehement recriminations on the part of England.

Finally, to state everything, although the report is guaranteed by nothing more than the affirmations of several natives, half an hour after the departure of the projectile a number of people in Goree and Sierra Leone claimed to have heard a muffled boom, the last remnant of sound waves which had crossed the Atlantic and come to die on the coast of Africa.

But we must return to Florida. When the first movement of tumult had passed, the whole crowd, including even the injured and deafened, shook off its torpor, and frenzied shouts of "Hurrah for Ardan! Hurrah for Barbicane! Hurrah for Nicholl!" rose up to the skies. Several million people, forgetting their contusions and consternation and thinking only of the projectile, looked up into space through telescopes and binoculars. But they looked in vain: the projectile was no longer in sight. They had to resign themselves to waiting for telegrams from Longs Peak. Mr. Belfast, the director of the Cambridge Observatory, was at his post in the Rocky Mountains. This skilled and persevering astronomer had been given the task of observing the projectile.

But an unforeseen, though easily foreseeable phenomenon, about which nothing could be done, soon put the public's patience to a harsh test.

The clear weather suddenly changed: the sky darkened and became covered with clouds. How could it have been otherwise, after the terrible displacement of atmospheric layers, and the dispersion of the enormous quantity of vapor that came from the explosion of 400,000 pounds of guncotton. The whole natural order had been disturbed. There is nothing surprising about this, since it has often been observed that the weather can be abruptly modified by the firing of big guns in a naval battle.

The next day the sun rose above a horizon laden with thick clouds, a heavy, impenetrable curtain between the sky and the earth. Unfortunately it extended all the way to the Rocky Mountains. It was a disaster. A chorus of protests arose from all over the globe. But nature paid no heed to it; since men had troubled the atmosphere with their detonation, they would have to take the consequences.

During this first day, everyone tried to see through the thick clouds, but to no avail. Furthermore, everyone was mistaken in looking up, for as a result of the earth's rotation the projectile was now moving away from the antipodes.

When deep, impenetrable darkness enveloped the earth and the moon rose above the horizon, it could not be seen; it seemed to be deliberately hiding from the audacious men who had shot at it. No observations were possible, and telegrams from Longs Peak confirmed this regrettable fact.

The explorers had left at forty-six minutes and forty seconds past ten o'clock on the evening of December 1; if the experiment was successful, they would arrive on December 4 at midnight. The world resigned itself to waiting till then, especially since it would have been quite difficult to observe an object as small as the projectile under those conditions.

On December 4, between eight o'clock and midnight, it would have been possible to follow the path of the projectile, which would have appeared as a black dot on the bright surface of the moon. But the weather remained mercilessly cloudy. The public's exasperation knew no bounds. Some people went so far as to shout insults at the moon for not showing itself. A sad turn of events!

J. T. Maston went to Longs Peak in despair. He wanted to see for himself. He had no doubt that his friends had arrived safely. There had been no word that the projectile had fallen on any of the earth's continents or islands, and J. T. Maston refused to admit the possibility that it might have fallen into one of the oceans that cover three-quarters of the surfaces of the globe.

On December 5 the weather was still unchanged. The great telescopes of the Old World, those of Herschel, Rosse, and Foucault, were constantly aimed at the moon, for the weather was clear in Europe, but their relative weakness made any useful observation impossible.

December 6: same weather. Three-quarters of the world was consumed with impatience. Wild schemes were proposed for dissipating the clouds that had accumulated in the air.

On December 7 the sky seemed to change a little. There was hope, but it did not last long. By evening the thick clouds were again defending the starry firmament against all eyes.

The matter was now becoming serious. On December 11, at eleven minutes past nine in the morning, the moon was to enter its last quarter. After that it would be waning, and even if the sky should clear, the chances of observation would be greatly lessened, for the moon would show a constantly decreasing portion of its surface, and would finally become new: that is, it would rise and set with the sun, whose rays would make it invisible. It would not be full again until January 3, at forty-seven minutes past midnight, and observations could not be resumed until then.

The newspapers published these facts with endless commentaries, and did not conceal from the public that it would have to have angelic patience.

December 8: nothing. On the ninth, the sun came out briefly, as though to taunt the Americans. It was greeted with jeers; apparently offended by this reception, it was extremely stingy with its rays.

On the tenth, there was no change. J. T. Maston nearly went mad, and there were fears for his brain, which had hitherto been so well preserved beneath his rubber skull.

But on the eleventh a great tropical storm arose. Strong east winds swept away the clouds that had been piled up for so long, and that evening the half-consumed disk of the moon passed majestically among the bright constellations of the sky.

CHAPTER 28

A NEW HEAVENLY BODY

THAT SAME night, the exciting news that had been so impatiently awaited burst like a bombshell over every state in the Union, then raced across the ocean and sped along every telegraph wire in the world. The projectile had been sighted, thanks to the gigantic telescope on Longs Peak.

Here is the report drawn up by the director of the Cambridge Observatory. It contains the scientific conclusion of the Gun Club's great experiment.

> *Longs Peak, December 12*
> *To the staff of the Cambridge Observatory.*
>
> *The projectile launched by the cannon at Stone Hill was seen by J. M. Belfast and J. T. Maston on December 12, at 8:47 P.M., with the moon in its last quarter.*
>
> *The projectile has not reached its goal. It passed to one side of it, but near enough to be held by the moon's gravity. Its rectilinear motion was changed to an extremely rapid circular motion. It has now become a satellite of the moon and is moving in an elliptical orbit around it.*
>
> *It has not yet been possible to ascertain the movements of this new satellite: neither its speed of*

*rotation nor its speed of revolution is known. Its
distance from the surface of the moon may be
estimated at approximately 2,830 miles.*

*There are two possibilities: either lunar gravity
will eventually draw the projectile to the surface of
the moon and the explorers will reach their
destination, or the projectile will be held in a fixed
orbit and will continue to move around the moon
until the end of time.*

*Observation will some day determine which is
the case, but so far the only result of the Gun Club's
project has been to add a new heavenly body to our
solar system.*

J. M. Belfast

What a multitude of questions this unexpected outcome
raised! What mysteries lay in store for scientific investi-
gation! Thanks to the courage and devotion of three men,
the enterprise of sending a projectile to the moon, which
at first might have seemed somewhat frivolous, had been
an enormous result whose consequences were incalculable. Although the explorers, imprisoned in their new
satellite, had not reached their goal, they were at least
part of the lunar world: they were circling the moon and,
for the first time, human eyes were able to penetrate all its
mysteries. The names of Nicholl, Barbicane, and Ardan
would be forever famous in the annals of astronomy, for
those bold explorers, eager to broaden human knowledge,
had fearlessly flung themselves into space and risked
their lives in the strangest undertaking of modern times.

When the Longs Peak report became known, there was
a feeling of surprise and fear all over the world. Was it
possible to go to the aid of those brave inhabitants of the
earth? No, because they had placed themselves outside of

mankind by going beyond the limits which God had imposed on earthly creatures. They had enough air for two months and enough food for a year. But afterward? Even the most insensitive hearts palpitated at this terrible question.

There was one man who would not grant that the situation was hopeless, who still had confidence. That man was the explorers' devoted friend, as daring and resolute as they were: the brave J. T. Maston.

He was keeping his eye on them. His residence was now the Longs Peak station, his horizon was the mirror of the huge reflector. As soon as the moon rose each night, he framed it in the field of the telescope, kept it in sight at every moment and assiduously followed it in its movement through space. With unremitting patience he watched the projectile pass across its silvery surface, and thus he remained in constant communion with his three friends, whom he still hoped to see again some day.

"We'll communicate with them," he said to anyone who would listen, "as soon as circumstances permit. They'll hear from us and we'll hear from them! I know them: they're ingenious men. Among the three of them they've taken into space all the resources of art, science, and industry. With that, you can do anything you want! They'll find a way, you'll see!"

ASK YOUR BOOKSELLER
FOR THESE BANTAM CLASSICS

THE HOUSE OF MIRTH, Edith Wharton, 978-0-553-21320-1
SUMMER, Edith Wharton, 978-0-553-21422-2
LEAVES OF GRASS, Walt Whitman, 978-0-553-21116-0
THE PICTURE OF DORIAN GRAY AND OTHER WRITINGS, Oscar Wilde,
    978-0-553-21254-9
THE SWISS FAMILY ROBINSON, Johann David Wyss, 978-0-553-21403-1
EARLY AFRICAN-AMERICAN CLASSICS, edited by Anthony Appiah,
    978-0-553-21379-9
FIFTY GREAT SHORT STORIES, edited by Milton Crane,
    978-0-553-27745-6
FIFTY GREAT AMERICAN SHORT STORIES, edited by Milton Crane,
    978-0-553-27294-9
SHORT SHORTS, edited by Irving Howe, 978-0-553-27440-0
GREAT AMERICAN SHORT STORIES, edited by Wallace & Mary Stegner,
    978-0-440-33060-8
AMERICAN SHORT STORY MASTERPIECES, edited by Raymond Carver &
    Tom Jenks, 978-0-440-20423-7
SHORT STORY MASTERPIECES, edited by Robert Penn Warren,
    978-0-440-37864-8
THE VOICE THAT IS GREAT WITHIN US, edited by Hayden Carruth,
    978-0-553-26263-6
THE BLACK POETS, edited by Dudley Randal, 978-0-553-27563-6
THREE CENTURIES OF AMERICAN POETRY, edited by Allen Mandelbaum,
    (Trade) 978-0-553-37518-3, (Hardcover) 978-0-553-10250-5